SNOW
IN
LOVE

OTHER BOOKS YOU'LL ENJOY:

SNOW
IN
LOVE

FOUR STORIES

MELISSA DE LA CRUZ ✳ **NIC STONE**
AIMEE FRIEDMAN ✳ **KASIE WEST**

POINT

Library of Congress Cataloging-in-Publication Data available

ISBN 978-1-338-31018-4

10 9 8 7 6 5 4 3 2 1   18 19 20 21 22

Printed in the U.S.A.   23
First edition, November 2018

Book design by Yaffa Jaskoll

SNOW
IN
LOVE

SNOW AND MISTLETOE

BY KASIE WEST

DECEMBER 22, 4:50 P.M.

A sleepy Christmas song played on the speakers overhead as I finally stepped up to the next available rental car clerk. She didn't even try to put a friendly smile on her face. I supposed a day like today would take the customer service out of anyone.

"Hi," I said. "My flight was canceled. I need to rent a car."

"Credit card and ID, please."

I pulled out my license and slid it across the counter. "I don't have a credit card."

Well, technically I did. My parents had given me an emergency credit card but I knew if I used it now, a purchase text would flash on my mom's cell phone screen. It would say something like: *Amalie is in Denver when she should be in Italy——you know, that place she begged to go for an exchange year? The place you paid for her to go? The place she ran away from after four months instead of the scheduled nine because apparently she's not as strong as she thought?*

"Doesn't the airline pay for my rental since they canceled my flight?" I asked the clerk.

3

She laughed, but when she realized I was serious, she added sadly, "Oh, honey, no. They don't, not when it's weather related." She picked up my license and showed it to me as if I didn't know what was on it. "But you can't rent a car. You're only seventeen."

"Right . . . so I take it the airline won't pay for a hotel either." I had exactly nineteen dollars left after buying my plane ticket with the earnings from a side job I wasn't supposed to have. I could feel the rolled-up wad of cash in my pocket, digging into my thigh as if mocking me about how little it would buy.

"Next!" the lady called over my head and then handed me back my license. "Good luck."

Tears stung the back of my eyes as I gathered my things and walked away from the counter. Bing Crosby crooned overhead about snow and mistletoe, and for some reason that made me want to cry more. I had been in an airport or on a plane for the last sixteen hours. Denver was my second layover; I was only supposed to be here for forty-five minutes. Now, with the snowstorm, I'd already been here three times that long, and counting.

I tucked my wallet into my backpack and slung the bag onto my shoulder. I'd checked my suitcase back in Milan, and it now sat on a plane, apparently unable to be removed before the plane reached its destination. Hopefully, the weather would soon clear, and my suitcase and I would both fly that plane home to California.

I found an empty spot against the wall and slid down it until I sat on the floor. Would I be allowed to sleep in this rental car place? I pulled out my phone and stared at the screen. For the millionth time, I thought about texting my mom. But I wasn't desperate enough yet. A text message wasn't going to be how I told my mom I'd left the program in Milan early. I needed to show up on her doorstep in person and explain things. The magic of Christmas would save me from her wrath. She loved Christmas.

"Hey, I think I know you," a voice said above me. The statement surprised me, because I knew nobody in Denver, Colorado.

I looked up to see Sawyer Harris: my high school's senior class president, and winner of last year's best smile award. He was staring at me, proving why he had absolutely deserved that award.

"Hey," I managed after too long of a pause. "What are you doing here?"

"You know, just hanging out," he said, his eyes sparkling with humor.

"Right, you're stuck too." *Just put your foot in your mouth, Amalie, and wait for your brain to reinhabit your skull.* I wasn't even sure why I was acting so starstruck. I had never had a crush on Sawyer, unlike half the girls at school. Sure, he was cute and seemed nice, but he was completely out of my circle and I didn't have the desire to change that.

He nodded. "The weather was great for snowboarding, not so great for leaving. You heading home for Christmas?"

"Yep. Yes."

"You went somewhere for an exchange year or something, right?"

"How do you know that?" I blurted.

He flashed me the famous smile again. "Not too many people venture quite so far."

It didn't really answer my question, but I accepted it. "Yes . . . I ventured. Now I'm trying to get home. So, snowboarding? Here in Colorado? Or is this your layover?" *There, finally some understandable words.*

He pointed over his shoulder to nobody in particular. "Yeah, me and some friends were here snowboarding. You probably remember them from school. Logan Thompson and Wes Chan. Oh, and my older sister, Heather."

I started to nod. I did remember Logan . . . sort of. Then I shook my head with a laugh. "Not really. Sorry. We were in completely different friend pools. I'm actually surprised you remember *me.*" Finally, my brain was all the way back. No more stumbling stupidly over words. I blamed it on being tired and frustrated. I would blame this day for everything if I needed to. It was completely ruining my life right now.

"Of course I remember you. Your voice is like . . ." He trailed off.

"A car without a muffler? Heralding angels? Your sentence could've gone either way."

He laughed. "Sorry. It sounded cheesy in my head."

A guy with spiky black hair and brown eyes came up behind Sawyer. "S . . . U . . . V," the guy said, slapping Sawyer on the back with each letter. "With four-wheel drive. Let's do this thing."

Sawyer nodded down at me. "Wes, you remember . . ."

"Amalie," I finished for him. So Sawyer didn't remember me as well as he claimed.

"Amalie," Sawyer said. "I was getting there."

Right. I nodded a "hi" up at Wes. At this point I felt like it was too late to stand but my neck was starting to ache.

Wes shook his head. "Don't remember you at all."

"Don't feel bad," I said even though it was obvious he didn't. "I don't remember you either."

"No?" Sawyer said to Wes. "She goes to high school with us."

"Well, not this year," I said. Although I was about to change that. I wanted to finish out senior year back home.

Sawyer added, "You'd remember her if she sang."

"If she sang?" Wes frowned.

"I'm not going to sing," I said, seeing exactly where this conversation was headed.

"Fine. But her voice is like . . ."

After several seconds I said, "One day you might finish that sentence."

Sawyer laughed.

A tall and lanky guy with a crop of bright blond hair walked up, joining our group. "Let's go," he said to Sawyer and Wes. "We have a vehicle."

"Logan, this is Amalie," Sawyer said.

Logan nodded down to me.

"How did you guys get a car?" I asked. "The lady wouldn't rent me one."

"My sister," Sawyer explained. "She's twenty-one."

"Oh, nice."

Logan jerked his head toward the exit, and he and Wes left. I looked out the window, where snow was falling pretty heavily now. It was probably better that I didn't get a car; I wouldn't have felt confident driving in that.

"Be careful," I said to Sawyer, who was lingering behind.

He followed my gaze out the window. "Right now, the worst of the storm is north of here and headed this way. We think we can beat it."

"Utah's not just as bad?" They'd have to drive through a lot of Utah on the way home.

"It's a lot better than here. A day and half and we'll be home." He turned his phone toward me. Some weather app was open. It showed severe snow for the next four days in Denver. Then he swiped his finger across the screen and Utah weather appeared, with four days of only clouds. He shrugged. "All I know is that if I'm not home by Christmas my mom will kill me," he said.

My chest was tighter than ever. "This storm is going to hang around for four days?" I could be stuck here through Christmas?

"You could come with us," he said.

"What?"

"To Fresno. In the SUV. There's room."

"I'm sure your friends would love that."

"They wouldn't care. Trust me. And Heather would probably appreciate the company. She said something about our maturity level yesterday."

You shouldn't get in a car with someone you hardly know, I told myself. *No matter how desperate you are.* I didn't even know three facts about this guy. "I think I'll pass," I said.

"Okay." He gave me a small wave. "Hopefully you beat us home." He spun around and walked away. I watched him join up outside with Wes and Logan, and a girl who must've been his sister. She had his same sandy-brown hair and expressive brown eyes. I watched as she tied her wavy hair back into a ponytail. My own long dark hair felt matted and messy from all the travel.

My gaze drifted to Sawyer, who laughed at something Logan said.

Okay. He liked to snowboard. That was a fact I knew about him.

I bit my lip and played with the strap on my backpack as the group moved toward the sliding doors that led to the parking garage.

Oh, and he won that award for his smile last year. Fact.

I laced my fingers together, then pulled them apart again. "His last name is Harris," I whispered. I totally knew three facts about him. I jumped up.

"Sawyer, wait!"

DECEMBER 22, 6:15 P.M.

"**Y**ou look skeptical," Sawyer said as everyone piled into the SUV.

"I am."

He smiled. "A road trip can't be harder than a year in Italy."

I met his eyes and let out a little chuckle. He was right. The last four months had been hard.

Sawyer opened up the back of the SUV and threw in his large backpack. When I handed him mine he said, "Wow, you pack light."

"My luggage is on the plane. They wouldn't get it off for me."

"Was your life in there?" he asked.

"Pretty much."

He looked down at the jeans I was wearing and then my tee and hoodie. "You're going to be cold." He reached for his backpack, unzipped it, and pulled out a big ski jacket. "Here. You can use this."

"Is this all you packed?" I asked. "Because there is no way anything else can fit in that bag if this was in there."

I silently added *low maintenance* to facts I knew about Sawyer. Although maybe this meant he just never changed his clothes . . . or brushed his teeth.

"It has the ability to squeeze into small spaces."

"Thanks."

He slammed the hatch and opened the car door.

Heather, Sawyer's sister, was driving and Wes had claimed shotgun. Logan sat on the middle bench, his backpack taking up a seat and his long legs stretched out onto the other.

"I'll take the back," I said. Maybe that would make them feel better when I was the only one not contributing money for this ride.

I climbed in and Sawyer followed after me, to the last row.

"I can sit back here by myself," I said.

"Logan doesn't share well, so I'd already claimed the back," Sawyer explained.

I wasn't sure if he was saying that to be nice, or if he really did claim the back (who claims the back?), but I didn't feel like I could argue about it.

The second I was sitting down, with my seat belt on and my headrest adjusted, I knew quite definitely that I was not going to be good company. I was T-minus five minutes away from being dead to the world.

"Let's beat this storm!" Wes said from the front.

The others cheered their agreement.

"I'm sorry," I said to Sawyer.

"Why?"

"I've been up for almost twenty-four hours."

"Oh, is that what the slightly glazed look is in your eyes?"

"That or the drinks I stole from the bar cart on the last leg," I said, my eyelids going heavy.

"Really?"

"No, it was a joke. I don't mess with airport security. They're like their own sovereign nation. A nation of tyranny and chaos." I wasn't sure what I was saying anymore. I was rambling.

"Tyranny and chaos? Aren't those the opposite of each other?"

"I think you might be right. One is absolute rule, one is a lack of order. But somehow, the airport brings these two together and makes them coexist in complete and utter disharmony."

He smiled. "You *are* tired."

My eyes went to his bright smile. "I think you *do* brush your teeth."

Now he laughed. "I have a feeling I could ask you anything right now and you'd tell me the truth. This could be trouble."

I leaned my head against the window. "I am about to be in a huge amount of trouble." At home, that was. And I had a day and a half to prepare for it.

DECEMBER 22, 9:45 P.M.

Something smelled good. Like pine or soap or clean. It must've been the laundry detergent from the pillow I was sleeping on.

No, because I was on a seat, my legs on the floor, but the rest of my body twisted awkwardly across cold leather. In a car, I suddenly remembered. I felt wetness on my cheek and realized that was from me . . . drooling. My eyes flew open. I was lying on someone's legs.

The events that led me here came back in a flash. I wiped at my cheek and sat up. The car glowed red from brake lights in front of us. Aside from that, it was dark. The day had passed to night with me asleep on Sawyer's legs. The rest of the car was quiet, except for some news station Heather had on the radio. Wes and Logan were sleeping; maybe Sawyer was asleep too. Maybe he had no idea I had drooled on his leg for the last however many hours. I bit my lip and turned to check.

He wasn't asleep.

"I'm sorry about your leg," I said.

He gave me a half smile. "Wes once spit in my soda. That was worse."

My mouth dropped open.

"I mean, way worse," he said, backtracking. "That wasn't a good comparison."

I laughed. "It's fine. I deserve it." I nodded toward his leg. "Thank you for letting me sleep."

Heather turned in her seat. "We've gone sixty miles in three hours."

"What?" I asked. "That's not good."

"No, it's not. I've been following this semi because it's making really good tire tracks in the snow for me, but it's slow going. And it's ten o'clock and I'm about to die of boredom, so someone needs to entertain me before I fall asleep."

"So about that one and a half days to get home . . ." Sawyer said.

"Is it too late to go back to the airport and wait it out?" I asked.

"Absolutely," Heather said.

"I still stand by my claim that we will beat your airplane," Sawyer told me. "We are actually moving."

Heather let out a breath between her lips as if protesting that statement.

"Do you want me to drive, Heather?" Sawyer asked.

"Funny," she said darkly.

"It wasn't a joke," he said.

"There is no way I'm going to let any seventeen-year-old drive this car. It is a rental. There is a snowstorm outside. You will wreck it, and I will have to pay thousands of dollars I don't have because I let someone not allowed to drive, drive."

Sawyer held up his hands. "I was just offering."

"Even if you were allowed to drive, I wouldn't let you. I saw how you drove that snowmobile this weekend. You were horrible. Not as bad as Wes, but I'd be crazy to trust you with my life."

"Amalie can drive," Sawyer said. "I bet she is an excellent driver."

"Amalie, are you older than seventeen?" Heather asked me, glancing in the rearview mirror.

"No," I said.

"Then my original statement still applies." She reached down and turned up the radio. A story about the storm had just come on. "Shhh. Hold on."

I turned to Sawyer. "You would place a bet on my driving skills when you know nothing about me?" I asked quietly.

"I know a few things about you."

He didn't even know my name before today, so I doubted it. "Like what?"

He started to answer and I interrupted with, "Aside from the singing thing."

"And the Italy thing?" he reminded me.

"Right." Those were two big public things that people had probably talked about at school.

"What are you guys saying back there?" Heather asked.

"We're talking about how Amalie knows nothing about me," Sawyer said.

"I can fix that. I know everything worth knowing about Sawyer." Heather smacked Wes on the arm, waking him up. "We're playing a game."

"We are not playing a game," Sawyer said.

Wes sat up from where he'd been sleeping against the window. He ran his hand through his already spiky black hair, making it spikier. He looked around in confusion before saying, "What?"

"I need entertainment so I don't fall asleep," Heather told him.

"What did you have in mind?" Wes asked in a flirty voice.

She put her hand up. "Not whatever you're thinking. It's time to share Sawyer facts."

"What are those?" Wes asked.

"It is not time to share anything," Sawyer said.

Heather ignored him. "We each say something true about Sawyer. Wake up Logan."

Wes started throwing things at Logan: the rental car pamphlet, a sock, a beanie. Logan first kicked up one of his legs, as if that would stop the assault. When Wes didn't give up, Logan's blond head finally appeared above the seat, the only thing I saw at first, before he dragged the rest of his body into a sitting position.

"We're sharing facts about Sawyer," Wes said.

"Heather, if it's facts you want, I have some fun ones about you," Sawyer said.

I smiled. "That's a good idea. I'm in a car with four strangers; I'd like to know about all of you."

"Fine," Heather said. "We can each share one fact about anyone in this car that is not ourselves."

"I'll start," Wes said, raising his hand. "Sawyer once stole a pack of gum from a homeless man."

I raised an eyebrow at Sawyer.

He immediately protested, "No, no, that's not—"

"That's exactly what happened," Wes interrupted.

"And what about that time when Sawyer snowboarded in his underwear?" Logan chimed in.

"Um, what?" I asked.

"Those were both dares!" Sawyer exclaimed.

Logan nodded. "Sawyer never backs down from a dare. Another important fact."

Wes held up his finger. "Except that one time—"

"We are supposed to be sharing facts about everyone in this car," Sawyer said. "And I wouldn't exactly call these things *facts* about me. They are *events.*"

Heather patted the steering wheel. "Sawyer likes spicy food."

"There," Sawyer said. "That's better."

"Sawyer once ate two of those really hot peppers and cried," Wes said.

"And then vomited," Logan added.

I laughed, but then put on a sympathetic face when I realized that probably wasn't an appropriate reaction.

"Or remember when Sawyer laced Heather's burger with hot Cheetos?" Wes asked with a grin.

"Events! These are events!" Sawyer cried. "And not even events. These are things you guys dared me to do. They probably say more about you than they do about me."

"You laced my burger with hot Cheetos?" Heather asked. "When?"

"It didn't faze you at all," Wes said.

"Huh," Heather muttered. "I knew I shouldn't trust teenagers around my food."

"Heather, you are four years older than us," Sawyer said. "You were a teenager literally two years ago."

"Sawyer is right," Heather said. "I'd say these qualify more as stories than 'getting to know a person' facts. So dig a little deeper, boys."

"About other people in this car," Sawyer said, then added to me, "I'm really not as irresponsible as they're making me seem."

"Yes, Sawyer gets straight As," Logan teased like this was a bad thing. "And he reads too much. For fun."

"He once won a hot dog eating contest," Wes said, unable, it seemed, to steer clear of events and focus on personality.

"That's true," Sawyer said as if this was the first thing said that he was proud of.

"Then he barfed," Logan added.

"You seem to throw up a lot," I said.

"I think it's my choice in friends."

"Yes, Sawyer is very loyal," Heather said. "Regardless of how dumb his friends are."

"So loyal that he's had a crush on the same girl since the ninth grade," Wes said.

"I think that means I'm pathetic," Sawyer said. "Is it someone else's turn yet? I have some facts. Wes once ate an entire tube of toothpaste and his mom made them pump his stomach. And Logan plays the guitar like Santana, despite his extra-long limbs, and can solve a Rubik's Cube in two minutes. And Heather practically raised me." That last one seemed to catch him off guard. Like he hadn't meant to say it. He quickly added, "I mean, she's like a second mom or whatever."

Heather met his eyes in the rearview mirror and said incredulously, "You've had a crush on the same girl since the ninth grade?"

He rolled his eyes. "No."

"But what about Candice and Paige and what's her name? That girl you dated sophomore year," she said.

Lisa. He'd dated Lisa our sophomore year. I didn't realize I'd remembered her name until that moment. I'd seen them holding hands around campus. I knew Candice too, but I didn't know Sawyer had dated her. Maybe he'd dated her *this* year. Or maybe I hadn't noticed. We ran in different circles, after all.

"Exactly," Sawyer said. "Wes was exaggerating. Like he always does."

"It's called pining," Wes said. "And your brother is very good at it. Add that to the list of personality traits."

"Whatever," Sawyer grumbled.

"And you've never told me about this?" Heather asked Sawyer. "No wonder nothing has happened. You've had these idiots giving you advice. It's your lucky car trip, brother, you have two women in this car who are about to impart all their wisdom upon you. Right, Amalie?"

"Absolutely," I said.

"What have you done so far to win this girl's heart?" Heather asked as we inched forward on the highway.

"A lot of pining," Wes said. "And he talked to her at school a couple times, and at a party once."

I laughed. "Have you asked her out?"

Sawyer shook his head. "I'm just supposed to march up to her and say, 'do you want to go out with me?'"

"Yes," I said. "If you can snowboard in your underwear, this shouldn't be that hard. Wait . . . did this snowboarding event happen this last weekend?"

Wes whooped.

"You see what I've been dealing with?" Heather asked me.

"I'm sorry," I said.

"This is different than a stupid dare," Sawyer said. "This is . . ."

"The risk of rejection?" Heather offered.

"For starters."

"I think most girls just want a guy who is straightforward and honest," I said.

"But," Heather said, "if that's too hard for my apparently wimpy brother, there's nothing wrong with easing into it. A few casual conversations."

"It's not like I see her all the time," Sawyer argued. "And now it's winter break."

"That's it!" I said, shaking his shoulder. "Christmas."

"What about Christmas?"

"Get her a gift. Take it to her. I know that's more than a casual conversation but it's less than asking her out. It's just an 'I've been thinking about you.'"

"'For the last three years,'" Wes added. "'Please don't find me creepy.'"

I waved off Wes. "Don't listen to him. It's cute. It's thoughtful. She'll like it."

"I agree," Heather said. "It's innocent enough that you can talk your way out of it if it's obvious she doesn't like you back, and forward enough that you'll be able to tell if she does."

Sawyer nodded slowly. "I guess I can try that. And for the record, I have not been thinking about her for the last three years. Just occasionally, when I see her."

Wes cleared his throat as if about to protest but didn't.

"Good," Logan said. "That's solved. Now, we've been in here for four hours. Can we make a pit stop? Or I might have to pee out the window."

Heather grunted. "I have no doubt you would, but yes, I'll stop at the next gas station."

DECEMBER 22, 10:42 P.M.

"**W**e've gone eighty miles," Heather said when she pulled into a parking space at the gas station. "Over a thousand to go."

When I climbed out of the car and the cold air bit at my cheeks, I reached back inside and grabbed Sawyer's ski jacket.

"Italy's a lot warmer than this?" Sawyer asked as we walked into the well-lit and nearly empty food mart.

A clerk stood at the counter and glared at us as the doors opened, like we had just filled his store with piles of snow.

My mind wandered back to walking the streets of Milan: the amazing architecture, the art, the food, the sun on my face. "It is warmer," I answered, feeling a wave of sadness. I would miss it there. But not enough to want to go back.

Logan ran straight for the bathroom and the rest of us headed toward the food aisle. On the way, Heather was distracted by the souvenir aisle. She held up a Breckenridge, Colorado, T-shirt.

"Maybe you should buy your crush some gas station gifts," she said to Sawyer with a smirk. "It might be all you have time to get before Christmas."

I started to laugh but then said, "Wait, that's not a bad idea!" I glanced at Sawyer. "It can be like a little story of your journey. You get something at each stop. Then you can tell her all about your trip home."

Heather put her hand on her heart. "Your journey to her."

"I sense you are both now mocking me," Sawyer said.

"You just now sensed that?" Wes asked.

"We're not mocking you," I said, holding up a snow globe of Denver and giving it a shake. "Well, not a lot."

"I vote for this fake gold medal." Wes held it up. "It's like you're saying, *you won . . . me.*"

Sawyer cursed us all under his breath but then walked farther into the souvenir aisle.

I tried not to laugh and put the snow globe back on the shelf. I watched as the tiny white flakes settled around the buildings.

"My dad used to bring me home snow globes from wherever he went," I said to Heather, who was digging through a basket of pins.

"Oh yeah? What does your dad do?" Heather asked.

"Ag stuff. He teaches farming seminars. What does your dad do?"

"He's a pilot. It's actually how we got to fly to Colorado. And how we knew that we'd all be trapped at the airport for days."

I ran my hand over another snow globe. "I better find the bathroom before we go."

When I came out of the bathroom, I searched for some food that was cheap, yet filling. If this trip was going to take us more than a couple days, I needed to conserve my money. I found a pastry and the cheapest bottle of water and made my way to the register.

Sawyer's stuff was being bagged and Wes, Logan, and Heather were getting ready to head out.

"What did you end up getting?" I asked Sawyer.

"None of you deserve to know that because of all your mocking," he said loudly for everyone to hear. He swiped the bag off the counter, gave me a wink, and followed the others out the door.

The thought of picking up cheesy Christmas gifts at each of our stops sounded so fun to me that I wished I had more money. As it was, I was going home empty-handed. It would be the first year in a while that I hadn't gotten my parents or younger brother something for Christmas. I felt terrible. I would be showing up present-less, having left my exchange year early. My family might be happy to see me for a minute, but then I'd probably end up ruining Christmas.

I took my bag and walked outside. Wes was holding a big garbage can lid and pointing to a snowy hill behind the gas station.

"What's going on?" I asked as Sawyer grabbed the lid and took off running.

"Some sort of dare," Heather said with a sigh.

The two of us stood and watched as Sawyer stretched out across the garbage can lid and slid down the hill of snow headfirst. Logan and Wes whooped.

"Good for you!" Heather shouted. "Now come on!"

DECEMBER 23, 1:03 A.M.

"**W**e should stop for the night," Sawyer said.

It was one in the morning, and it was obvious that Heather was having trouble staying awake. She'd downed a Mountain Dew after we left the gas station but she was fading fast.

The snow was coming down harder than before and we'd been following another semi for the last three hours. The truck had colorful lights strung along its tailgate, which seemed to be telling me that this was how I was going to spend my Christmas.

"The whole point of leaving the airport was to get ahead of the storm," Heather said. "If we stop now, we might as well have stayed. The snow will catch up with us."

Sawyer was staring at his phone and since he didn't argue with her, I assumed what Heather had said was right—we needed to keep going. "Amalie agreed to sing us some songs to keep you awake, then," he finally said.

My heart seemed to stop in my chest even though I knew he was kidding. I managed to cough out a little laugh, hoping that would be enough to get the subject dropped.

"That's right!" Heather exclaimed. "You said something about being a singer earlier."

I had? I guess I'd mentioned it when I was talking to Sawyer.

"And Italy," Heather said. "Is that why you were in Italy? For singing?"

The answer to that question was yes. My voice had been my ticket to Italy; I'd been accepted to a school for developing singers.

"It was just one of those exchange programs. Lots of people do them," I said as my answer. I hadn't even told my parents that I'd left, let alone why I'd left. I wasn't telling this car first.

"When do you have to go back?" Sawyer asked. He was digging through his bag from the gas station. He pulled out a package of trail mix and opened it.

"Back?" I asked.

He nodded, his mouth full of mixed nuts. "For the rest of your exchange year. You're just home for the holidays, right?"

"Oh . . . um . . . I don't remember the exact date." What was the exact date of never?

"If I can change the radio station, I will sing anything you want, Heather," Wes said.

"Is that a promise or a threat?" Heather asked.

Wes switched the station away from the news and started singing Pearl Jam at the top of his lungs. Heather joined in on the chorus and soon the whole car was singing badly, even though no one but Wes knew the lyrics.

I mouthed along, hoping Sawyer wouldn't call me out.

It wasn't that I couldn't sing *at all* now. It was only when people were paying attention that my throat seemed to freeze up, as cold as the air outside. Back in Italy, I had seen the school doctor and the school therapist and had analyzed myself extensively. It came down to the pressure of being away from home and the intense competition of the program.

I had thought I was stronger than that. My whole future, the one I'd dreamt of for the last five years, was gone. Who would hire an opera singer who couldn't hold up under pressure?

DECEMBER 23, 7:17 A.M.

As the morning sun crept over the mountains, we pulled into Grand Junction, Colorado. We still had nine hundred miles to go, but according to Sawyer's weather app, we'd passed the worst of the storm.

"Let's stop here for six hours," Heather said. "We'll leave after lunch. You can all find something to do because I am sleeping in this car alone."

"You want us to find something to do for six hours?" Sawyer asked.

"Did you sleep last night, Sawyer?"

"Yes, Heather," he said, humbled. We had all taken turns sleeping the night before. Except Heather. She deserved six hours of sleep alone in a car.

She drove into a parking lot in a small downtown area, parked, and turned off the car. "Come wake me up at noon." When none of us moved she added, "Run along and play, children."

I pulled on Sawyer's ski jacket, and we followed Logan and Wes out of the car. Snow crunched beneath our feet but nothing was falling from the sky at the moment.

The locks on the SUV clunked into place. When we all glanced back at Heather, she just waved and reclined her seat.

"Okay," Sawyer said, turning a full circle. "What should we do?"

Wes pointed. "Diner. Breakfast."

Nobody objected—except for the thirteen dollars and change in my pocket and the nineteen hours (assuming there was perfect weather and zero stops) it would take to get home from here. The guys just trudged forward. I lingered behind.

Sawyer turned and walked backward. "You coming?"

"I'll meet up with you guys later. I'm just going to look around."

"Aren't you hungry?"

Starving. "I'm okay." I wondered if there was a grocery store somewhere close. My money would go further there.

Sawyer shrugged and caught up with the others. I pulled out my phone and searched for a nearby grocery store. The closest one was over three miles away. Not helpful. My next search was for a McDonald's. I could get two Egg McMuffins for three bucks. My phone showed me that was even farther.

I looked one way down the street and then the other, then zipped up my overly large jacket. I'd find something.

The store windows were decorated for the holidays, with colorful scenes painted on the glass or wintertime displays. Christmas music drifted out of doors as people entered and exited. I found myself humming familiar tunes as I walked.

My Converse were not made for snow. They were made for airports and airplanes and Italy and . . . Fresno. By the time I'd walked several blocks, my socks were soaked through, but no good food options had presented themselves. This was a place full of specialty shops and boutiques, small candy stores, and ice cream parlors. It wasn't a place for a budget-conscious tourist.

I turned around and headed back toward the diner. I could find something cheap to eat there. On my way, I noticed a small shop full of Christmas decorations. I couldn't help myself; I stepped inside.

The warm air made my numb cheeks sting. The smell of cinnamon and pine and oranges filled the entire shop, and an intense bout of homesickness nearly knocked me off my feet. This was what Christmas smelled like in our home. My mom would simmer cinnamon sticks and sliced oranges on the stove, and the scent seeped into every corner of the house. We always got a freshly cut pine tree that we'd decorate together the day after Thanksgiving. Every year, we'd each pick out one new ornament to add to the tree.

This was the first year I'd missed that. I walked slowly around the store, taking everything in. I wanted to pick out an ornament, give it to my mom for Christmas, but the cheapest one I could find was fifteen dollars.

The woman behind the counter smiled at me as I passed her. "Can I help you find anything?" she asked.

"Just looking. It smells so good in here."

"Thank you." She pointed to a bin of square envelopes by the register. "They're little potpourri packs. Five dollars each if you're interested."

I picked one up and smelled it, again hit by a wave of nostalgia. "Five dollars." I ran my hand over the pocket of my jeans, bit my lip, and then nodded. "Sure. I'll take one." My mom would love this because it represented tradition. She'd see I'd been paying attention.

"Is that all? I'm not trying to rush you out of here or anything."

"That's all."

"Great." She rang me up and handed me the bag.

A little fir tree sat by the register and as I was about to leave, an ornament caught my eye. A silver bird.

"She's pretty, isn't she?" the lady asked.

"Gorgeous." My mom used to call me her songbird when I was little. I hadn't remembered that in a while. I nodded at the lady behind the counter. "Thank you."

"Merry Christmas."

I reached the door just as the guys burst into the store with a gust of cold air and laughter.

"Amalie," Sawyer said when he saw me. "Hey."

Wes and Logan waved but continued into the store.

"Hi. How was breakfast?" I asked Sawyer.

"Too much food."

My stomach let out a little gurgle that only I heard.

"Oh, speaking of." He thrust a small Styrofoam box toward me. "You want my leftovers? I'm not sick or anything."

"Thank you, I was just about to look for something to eat."

"I saved you, then."

"For sure." He had no idea just how much.

I found a bench outside, next to a large bike made of iron that was bolted to the ground. I opened the small box to see what Sawyer had ordered for breakfast: eggs and bacon. I was glad nobody was around to see me eat it with my fingers.

❋   ❋   ❋

My still-wet socks were beginning to turn my toes into icicles when the guys came out of the store.

"It's not exactly a bike for riding," Sawyer was saying.

"That's why it's a dare," Wes responded as if this was obvious.

Sawyer circled the bicycle. The wheels were taller than he was. He gave it a shake to ensure it was securely bolted. "Fine." He handed the couple bags that he was holding to Logan.

"Are you always the daree and never the darer?" I asked Sawyer.

"It seems that way," he said.

"Oh, please," Wes said. "Don't fall for his 'poor me' act. He's dished out just as much as he's taken."

Sawyer laughed, planted his foot on an iron spoke, and swung his leg up and over the seat. "There," he said. "Done."

"Not yet," Wes said. "Say it."

"You guys are jerks, you know that?" Sawyer said.

"Say it."

He let out a huge sigh, then yelled, "Look at me, I'm a little boy on a big bike!"

A couple who had been walking by turned and scowled at him. I could feel my own face heating up even though Sawyer didn't seem embarrassed at all.

The memory of my last time standing on the stage at school in Milan washed over me. My throat tightened, like it thought I was going to try to sing and it was once again refusing me. I clenched my teeth.

Sawyer jumped off the bike and plopped onto the bench next to me.

"I don't know if I want to be seen with you," I said through my tight throat.

"I understand."

Wes pointed down the street. "I saw a candy store up there. Should we check it out?"

"Go ahead. I'll catch up," Sawyer said.

Logan handed Sawyer back his bags and the guys took off, kicking snow at each other the whole way down the street.

"You can say it," Sawyer said.

"What?"

"We're immature."

"As long as you know."

Sawyer studied my face for a moment. "Are you okay?"

"I'm fine." My expression must've shown my unwanted memory.

"What did you buy?" he asked, nodding toward the bag on my lap.

"Christmas."

"You bought Christmas? That sucks for the rest of us."

"It really does." I opened the bag and held it out to him. "Smell."

"Smell?"

"I dare you," I said in a deep-voiced impersonation of Wes.

"Ouch." Sawyer grabbed at his chest. "But you know me, I can't turn one of those down." He leaned over the bag and took a whiff. "Oh," he said in surprise. "That *is* Christmas."

I smiled. "What about you? What did you buy?"

"I bought a scarf for my mom and another gift for you-know-who."

"Your crush?"

"Yep."

I felt a prickle of curiosity. "Wait, *do* I know her?" I asked.

"She goes to our school," he said.

"The one I haven't been to since June?"

"Yes, that one."

But I'd been going there for the three years before that. "Well?"

"Well, what?"

"What's her name?"

He let out a single laugh. "I'm not telling you that. I have to save some face in case she rejects me."

Who might Sawyer like? I tried to picture some of the girls on the periphery of his friend group. Maybe Lani? I had once seen them talking in the cafeteria and she was beautiful.

"Oh." Sawyer reached into his bag. "And I bought these." He pulled out a pair of socks and handed them to me.

"You bought these for me?"

"Converse aren't great in the snow."

"You're very observant. I'll add that to the list of facts I've learned about you." And thoughtful. He was definitely thoughtful.

"What about you?" he asked.

"What do you mean?"

"It hasn't escaped my notice that the only person we learned facts about in the car yesterday was me. So you owe me a few facts about yourself."

I smiled and shook my head. "You had the advantage of other people listing facts about you. It's much harder to think of interesting facts about myself on the spot like this."

"Okay, fair enough. How about you tell me when you think of some?"

"Deal."

DECEMBER 23, 1:25 P.M.

"**H**ow was your nap?" Sawyer asked his sister as we pulled back onto the freeway.

"Better than nothing," Heather answered. "The important thing is that the snow stayed away."

"We're not supposed to have any more snow now," Sawyer said, checking his weather app. "We already beat it."

"I hope so."

DECEMBER 23, 2:30 P.M.

"**S**awyer," Heather said an hour later. "What do you call white stuff that falls down from the sky?"

I peered out the window. We'd made it through a red rocky canyon and into Utah when the flakes started floating down. Soft at first, harmless, and then whipping around the car like they wanted to carry us off the road.

"I have no service right now," Sawyer replied with a straight face. "I'm not sure what that stuff is without the internet to tell me."

"Very funny," Heather said. "Add a couple more hours to the trip, people."

"We're never getting home," Wes said. "We're going to have to become one with nature and live amongst the rocks."

"Can you all keep it down?" Logan said. "I'm trying to nap."

This set off a series of screams from Heather and Wes.

"Did you call your parents at our last stop?" Sawyer asked me in the chaos.

"No. I'm surprising them."

"They don't know you're coming home for Christmas?"

"Oh, is that what a surprise means? Never mind."

He smiled. "And you haven't seen each other in four months?"

"No."

"Are you excited?"

I was both excited and terrified. "Beyond."

"Are you surprising your friends too?"

"Nobody knows I'm coming."

"What was the school in Italy like?"

"It was really cool. There were people from all over the world and we met in this really old building with hand-painted tile floors and mosaics on the walls." I paused. "And it was . . . much harder than I thought it would be."

"Wait, do you speak Italian?" Sawyer asked.

"I thought I did. But then I showed up there and learned very quickly that I don't speak it well. Some of the classes were in English though, so that was nice."

"How did you learn Italian?" Sawyer asked. "Our school doesn't offer it as a language choice."

"I wanted to be an opera singer. Most operas are in Italian."

"Wanted to be?"

"Want to be," I corrected hurriedly. "So when I was ten, my parents found a private tutor and I've been taking lessons ever since."

"Wow. And you didn't think that was an interesting fact you could share?"

"I told you I would share the facts as they came to me."

"True, but if the fact that you speak a second language isn't just sitting there waiting to be bragged about, I'm not sure that you know yourself at all."

I sort of agreed with that statement—I wasn't sure I did know myself, and maybe it had taken me going to Italy to realize it. "I told you, I don't speak it that well. It's not a bragging point."

"It is. Put that one on the list of things you share in the first five minutes of talking about yourself." He held up a clear plastic bag that he had filled in the candy store earlier, when we'd joined up with Logan and Wes. "Another fact, almost equally as interesting would be: What is your favorite candy?" He tilted the bag toward me.

"I take it yours is anything gummy."

"Lucky guess."

I pulled out a green-and-white gummy worm from the sea of gummy bodies. "I'm actually more of a salty person."

"Interesting."

"Is it?"

He smiled. "For sure."

"Speaking of random interesting facts, can I ask you a question?"

"Anything," he said in a faux serious voice.

"How does a junior win one of those back-of-the-yearbook awards? I thought those were reserved for seniors."

"Is that even a real question? Have you *seen* my smile?" He put it on full display for me.

I laughed.

Logan, who must've been listening in on our conversation from where he was laid out on the seat in front of us, raised his hand. "He can thank me for that award."

"It was a dare," Sawyer said. "Wes dared Logan to put someone's name on the ballot and apparently there is not a good vetting process because my name got through to the voting round. But my smile did the rest, Logan."

"Of course it was a dare," I said.

"See," Heather said. "You're learning."

"I think Heather and Amalie are jealous of the dare stories we have," Wes said thoughtfully. "You need some stories of your own. I have a dare for you, Heather."

She glanced at him once, waiting for the challenge.

"I dare you to let me drive."

Heather laughed long and loud. When she stopped, she said, "The difference between me and you guys is that I don't need to prove myself in some weird way. I can just say no."

Wes threw a piece of candy at her—something small and red. "You're no fun."

"If it hadn't been for me, none of your parents would've let you go on this trip," Heather protested. "So I disagree. I am the most fun."

Sawyer whispered just loud enough for only me to hear. "I dare you to throw this gummy worm at the back of Wes's head."

Without a second thought, I grabbed the gummy worm and flung it at Wes. It hit him right in the temple, then landed on the center console.

"Sawyer, keep your candy to yourself." Wes picked up the gummy worm and ate it.

"That was Amalie," Sawyer said.

"Yeah right."

Sawyer looked at me as if I should fess up and I just gave him a shrug and a smile. It was a stupid, easy dare, but I had a feeling that Sawyer didn't think I would do it. But I had. And there was something very freeing about that.

DECEMBER 24, 12:01 A.M.

"It is the twenty-fourth of December, I declare only Christmas music to be sung or played from here on out." Heather changed the station as the clock on the dash clicked over to 12:01 a.m. Mariah Carey's voice rang out.

"Am I the only one awake?" Heather asked.

"Nope. I'm up," I said.

I waited for Sawyer to chime in that he was awake as well, but he said nothing. I glanced over to find him leaning his head against the window, his eyes closed.

"Just us, huh?" Heather said.

"Apparently."

"Have we all scared you yet?" Heather asked. "I know you weren't planning on more than a day with a bunch of strangers."

We passed a sign that said ten miles to Beaver, Utah. The last eight hours had only taken us another three hundred miles.

"I just spent a semester with a bunch of strangers, so this is nothing."

"They weren't strangers the entire semester though, right?" Heather asked.

"I got to know my roommate. She was nice." I would actually miss her. "But with a language barrier and the competitive nature of the school, a lot of times I felt very much . . ."

"Alone?"

"Yes." I swallowed hard.

Heather glanced at me in the rearview mirror. "I'm sorry."

"It's okay."

"Why was it so competitive?" she asked.

"Because we were literally competing for parts in showcases," I explained. "Scouts would come from different colleges to hear us. Scholarships were on the line." I twisted my hands in my lap, remembering. "I just needed to step away from it all, to see if it would help."

"Help with what?"

"Everything." But most of all my voice. My ability to perform.

"And how's it going so far? Your step away from it all?"

I considered this question. "Well, it would help if we weren't running away from snowstorms, but aside from that, it's actually been surprisingly . . . fun."

Heather laughed. "My brother has that effect on a lot of people. He's good at getting people out of their comfort zones, but in a comforting way."

"I can see that." That was the perfect way to describe him.

"It's because he's been there."

"Been where?" I asked.

"Inside of himself, wound tight, needing to let go of things he couldn't control."

"Is that where you think I am?" I asked.

"Isn't it?"

She could tell this from the front seat of a car, overhearing snippets of conversation? Or was I the picture of uptight? The picture of fear?

A peppy rendition of "Jingle Bells" came on the radio, startling me. At that same moment, Heather gasped. The car seemed to hydroplane across the road, sliding sideways before gaining traction again. I caught my breath, my heart pounding. None of the boys had woken up.

"That's it," Heather said firmly. "We're stopping for the night. It's way too icy out here."

DECEMBER 24, 12:48 A.M.

Heather found the first motel she could, and headed into the lobby to ask about vacancies. The rest of the car had woken when we'd pulled to a stop in the parking lot.

I sat nervously fidgeting for a while before I whispered, "Sawyer?"

He leaned closer. "Yeah?"

"I can't pitch in for the motel. I have like seven dollars to my name. I can pay you back later though."

"What? Oh. Don't worry about it. Look at this place." He gestured outside the window. "It's probably fifty bucks a night, tops."

"Thank you."

I could tell he wanted to ask me questions about my money situation but then Heather opened the car door, waved a key card, and said, "One room, two beds, one couch. We will deal with this like adults."

"But there's only one adult here," Wes said. "How are we supposed to do that?"

She chose to ignore him. "Everyone needs to schedule time for a shower because this car is getting ripe. We'll leave as soon as the sun heats up the road a bit."

She really was like a mini-mom.

We all piled out of the car and everyone gathered their luggage. I only had my backpack, which had next to nothing in it. Why had I packed all my toiletries in my check-on bag? I didn't even have a change of clothes.

Heather directed us up a set of stairs and she unlocked a door at the top. The room was so cold I could see my breath.

"I'll get the heat going," Sawyer said, finding the wall unit.

Heather flung her bag on the closest bed and looked at me. "Are you okay sharing with me or do you want the couch?"

"I'm okay sharing."

She went to the desk, grabbed a pen, and drew a grid on the top sheet of a pad of paper. "Fifteen-minute showers. Fifteen more minutes hanging out in the bathroom. Then your time is up. I get the first one so I can sleep after."

It was nearly one a.m. Which meant the last shift would be from three to three thirty. That was the shift I would take since I wasn't even paying for this.

Heather shut herself in the bathroom and Wes turned on the television. "We are not watching a weather channel," he preemptively said. "We are watching something festive."

"Festive?" Logan said. "What are you, ninety?"

Wes flipped through the channels until he came to a Claymation cartoon about a snowman.

"I'll be right back," Sawyer said.

"Are you checking to see if this place has a pool and a hot tub?" Wes asked.

"I'm going to see if they have a gift shop." He pulled the door shut behind him.

This wasn't exactly a five-star hotel. He'd be lucky to find a tube of toothpaste or a roll of Mentos.

I set my backpack on the bed and unzipped it, hoping to magically find the items that I knew I'd packed in my suitcase. My suitcase, still sitting on a plane. Or possibly already landed in Fresno.

The only thing in my backpack was a book I'd already read on the first leg of the trip, a pack of gum, a pair of headphones, and my passport. I made a mental note to always pack one change of clothes in my carry-on from now on.

The heater groaned menacingly but continued to putter out warm air. Ten minutes later, Sawyer knocked at the door.

Wes jumped off the bed, stood in front of the door, and called through it, "What's the secret password?"

"If you don't let me in, I'll shave your eyebrows in your sleep."

"Nope. It's only three words," Wes said.

"It's cold out here."

"That was four."

I stepped forward, pushed Wes out of the way, and unlocked the door.

Sawyer wrapped me in a cold hug, trapping my arms at my sides. "This girl is the only nice one in this room. Thank you, Amalie."

I laughed. "You're cold. Stop stealing my heat."

He immediately released me. And when he did, I noticed he held a small paper bag.

"You found what you were looking for?" I asked.

"Yes." He took the bag to his backpack and tucked it away in one of the side pockets.

"You know," I said. "As your mentor and the person who gave you the idea to give your crush gifts, I think I should probably have final gift approval to make sure you are picking out appropriate things."

"That's probably a good idea," Logan said.

"At this point," Sawyer said, "it's too late. These gifts are going to be between me and her."

A tinge of disappointment settled in my chest and I wasn't sure why.

"Oh!" Sawyer said, pulling something from his back pocket. "But I did get *you* this. You said all your toiletries were on the plane." He held a packaged purple toothbrush in his hand.

I closed my eyes in gratitude. "Thank you so much."

"It's really for all our sakes," Wes said.

This time I didn't need to be dared. I took off my shoe and chucked it at Wes.

DECEMBER 24, 2:50 A.M.

Sawyer was the second to last to shower. When he came out of the bathroom in a long-sleeved T-shirt and sweatpants, his hair wet, a trail of steam followed him. He'd only taken twenty minutes in there. Everyone else was asleep. The room was dark except for a single light on the desk, which was clicked onto its lowest setting.

I moved to take over the bathroom when Sawyer stopped me. "I left a clean T-shirt on the counter. If you want it, it's yours. I left some other toiletries in there as well. You're welcome to use them."

"I don't need to steal your stuff," I protested.

"Please do. I doubt we'll be stopping again for another shower before we make it home."

"Thank you."

"For getting you into this mess?" he asked.

"For being so nice." I held up my packaged toothbrush and slipped past him into the bathroom.

Everything was . . . wet. Like four other people had been using it for the last two hours. There was a single dry towel left and I was grateful for that.

I took my time in the shower, letting the heat relax all the tense muscles in my neck and back. When I was out, I brushed my teeth for much longer than the recommended two minutes. Then I pulled on Sawyer's T-shirt. It smelled clean, and it was big enough on me to double as a nightgown. When I went back into the room, the small light on the desk was now off but I saw a glowing light coming from inside the closet.

I walked over to the closet and saw that the door was cracked open and someone was sitting inside.

I slid the door open a little farther. Sawyer sat against the wall, several pillows behind him, reading a book by the light of his phone.

"What are you doing?" I whispered.

He looked up. "I took that late nap in the car, and I didn't want to disturb anyone."

I glanced over my shoulder at all the sleeping forms: Heather on one of the two beds, Logan on the floor, and Wes on the couch.

I looked back at Sawyer. He tugged a pillow out from behind his back, set it against the wall next to him, and scooted over a bit. It was his offer to join him. So I did. I stepped into the closet, slid the door closed behind me, and sat down next to him. It wasn't a huge closet, barely enough room for the two of us, side by side. Overhead two hangers formed another pair.

"Do you often read in closets?" I asked.

Sawyer grinned. "Surprisingly, this is my first time. You?"

"I can't say that I have. But I have sat in a closet before."

"Why?"

"Because sometimes it's the only place for privacy."

"As I've learned tonight."

"Until I interrupted you." He probably just wanted a minute alone. He'd been stuck in the back seat of a car with me nearly continuously for the last thirty-six hours. I moved to leave. "Sorry."

He grabbed my hand. "Stay."

I did. He kept hold of my hand, staring at it. My heart picked up speed and my cheeks warmed. Then I chastised myself. I didn't want to be a Candice or a Lisa or whoever else his sister mentioned that he'd dated, all the while thinking about his crush. Sawyer needed to let things play out with his crush before any other girl stood a chance. I gently took my hand back and adjusted the pillow behind me.

"When was the last time you sought refuge in a closet?" he asked.

I swallowed the lump that rose up in my throat at the memory. "Can I tell you something?"

"Of course."

I swallowed a couple more times. Here in this closet, in the middle of the night, memories swirling in my brain, I felt like I needed to talk. Get a bit of this out before I had to face my parents. "I dropped out of the program."

I don't know how I expected him to react—a gasp, a look of disappointment, a shocked grunt—but he just nodded slowly, like he somehow already knew this.

"Why?" he asked.

"I couldn't handle the pressure."

"The girl who can sing in front of a packed stadium at a football game couldn't handle pressure?"

"You saw that?"

"Yes."

"Wait, is that the only time you've ever heard me sing? With horrible sound equipment on a windy night?"

"Yes, but it was really good. Amazing."

I let out a scoffing sound.

"Until I have another performance to compare it to, I stand by my claim," he said.

I looked down. "That's the point, you won't. I can't sing anymore."

"You can't sing anymore?"

"Well, no . . . I mean, I can, just not in front of people, not when it matters."

"It only matters if people are listening?" he asked.

"For what I want to do, yes."

"Maybe . . ." He stopped and shook his head.

"What?" I asked. "Finish."

"Maybe if it started mattering when it was just for you again, then the rest would . . ."

"Would what? Just fall into place? The rest wouldn't matter? You're right, you've cured me." I could hear the anger in my voice. I was the one who asked him to finish his sentence and I was mad. The fact of the matter was that he was right. I had stopped appreciating music. I had forgotten why I loved it in the first place. It had become all about scoring a part. I still couldn't conjure up the feelings of joy I once had when only thinking about a piece of music. I leaned forward, burying my face in my knees.

"I'm sorry," he said. "You're right, I don't know anything about anything."

"I'm not mad at you," I said. "I'm mad at myself." And that was true.

"Maybe being home will help," he said.

I felt his hand tentatively touch my back, like he wanted to comfort me but wasn't sure how I would react. He really was a nice guy. If his crush rejected him, I was going to be so sad for him. He deserved the girl he wanted and she'd be lucky to have him.

"That's what I'm counting on," I said. "Home."

"And your parents? Are they going to be upset?"

"Yes. But after that. After the blowup, after the 'you have to get a job and pay us back your tuition' talk, then I'll be home." My shoulders relaxed a degree with just the thought. I was starting to believe that I would be fine once I was back in my familiar routines and surroundings.

Sawyer was quiet for a moment, then said, "If you ever need someone to practice singing in front of, I volunteer."

I turned my head so my cheek now rested on my knees and I could see him. "I might take you up on that if only to erase the last time you heard me from your ears. No wonder you couldn't think of an adjective to describe it before."

He met my eyes. "Gorgeous, perfect, heavenly."

If my face went red one more time, it was going to completely give away the fact that I'd joined the Sawyer fan club. I was developing a crush on this guy. And he had a backpack full of evidence that his heart was already taken. "Heavenly?" I repeated, trying to hide my embarrassment.

"Better than 'angelic.'"

"Barely."

He smiled, and then his face went serious. "You'll figure things out, Amalie. Sometimes you just have to let go for a little while."

I suddenly remembered what his sister had said in the car— about Sawyer understanding my situation. "Are you speaking from experience?" I asked.

"Long story that I've let go of." He gave me a smirk. "But it has to do with emotionally absent parents."

"I'm sorry."

He shrugged.

"If you ever need to share that long story, I'm a pretty good listener," I said.

"I'll listen to your songs and you'll listen to my sob stories? I think I got the better end of the deal, but I like this idea."

"Although, your new girlfriend might end up being the jealous type."

"True. She might be. That is, if this whole gift plan of yours works."

"It will," I assured him.

"I hope you're right," he said.

I hoped I was wrong, but I knew that was a very selfish thing to hope for, so I quickly made the opposite wish.

DECEMBER 24, 1:42 P.M.

"**A**rizona has never looked so good," Logan said the next afternoon, still bright-eyed and bushy-tailed from getting a good night's sleep on the motel room floor.

We were now nine hours from home. It was Christmas Eve. We'd make it to Fresno by Christmas. This thought made me happy.

"I know," Heather said. "It's so pretty and orange and dry."

Sawyer was asleep on my lap, his jacket beneath his head. We'd been up most of the night talking in that closet. I was trying my hardest not to move so he wouldn't wake up. I had been staring at him for the last hour and decided he was very pretty and that I was acting very creepy. Now I was trying not to stare at him. Instead, I was gently playing with his hair, which might have also been creepy, but I couldn't stop—his hair was wavy and soft.

"What about you, Amalie?" Heather asked.

"What?" Had they been talking to me?

"Any Christmas Eve traditions?" She met my eyes in the rear-view mirror and I could see that she was smiling. She knew. She could tell that I was crushing on her brother. I tried to put a casual expression on my face instead of the doe-eyed look that was surely there a moment ago.

"Um. Yes, we all exchange pajama gifts, and then we sleep in them that night," I said, feeling another pang of homesickness.

"That's fun," Heather said.

"What about you guys?" I asked.

"We exchange one gift, nothing specific though," she said. "And we eat lots of sugar."

"We do too." I smiled at the thought of my mom's Christmas cookies.

"We talk about past Christmas failures in an epic passive-aggressive showdown," Wes chimed in.

Heather shoved his shoulder. "Oh, come on. You have the best parents in the world."

"I don't know about the world, but they are pretty good."

"We go up to Shaver Lake and tube," Logan said. "I'm kind of glad I'm missing that right now because I'm so done with snow."

"I actually wouldn't mind a white Christmas," I said.

Everyone in the car groaned.

Sawyer stirred and I froze. His eyes fluttered open and he sat up with a stretch.

"Did I drool on you?" he asked, looking at my jeans. "Because that would be mortifying." He ran his hands through his hair and then over his face.

"Funny," I said.

"Amalie was just wishing for the impossible," Heather said.

"What's impossible?" he scoffed, as if he could grant any wish.

"Snow in Fresno."

"Oh, yeah, you might want to make a different Christmas wish." I met his eyes. "I'm working on that."

DECEMBER 24, 2:20 P.M.

"Logan, you have the bladder of a three-year-old," Heather said as she pulled off the freeway.

"I drink a lot of water. It's good for you. You all should learn from my example."

"'Mesquite, Nevada,'" Wes read a roadside sign out loud.

Heather parked in a gas station. "Don't touch any of the slot machines here, you underage children," she said, opening her door and jumping out.

When she shut the door, Wes turned and said, "Logan, I dare you to play one of the slot machines in the gas station."

"Why?" Logan asked. "If I win, I can't collect the money."

"Just to make Heather mad."

Logan seemed to think about this reasoning for a moment, then said, "Okay." Then he and Wes both hopped out of the car.

I laughed and glanced at Sawyer as we climbed out of the SUV. "So Wes actually dares Logan sometimes too."

"Wes dares whoever's name comes into his head first."

The air outside was warmer than it had been for the last several days. It felt good.

"Will you help me pick out a gift at this stop?" Sawyer asked, climbing out behind me.

"Yeah . . . sure," I said, trying to sound good-natured about it. *Don't be jealous*, I reminded myself.

The gas station store was decked out for the holidays. Colored lights were strung up and a lopsided Christmas tree was painted on the glass door. Inside, Logan was standing at the single slot machine by the front window. Wes was watching him, laughing, and Heather was giving them both her best "mom" look.

Sawyer and I wandered over to the souvenir aisle. Right away I saw a small stuffed blue bird and picked it up.

"You think I should get her that?" Sawyer asked.

"Oh." I turned the bird to face him. "No, my mom used to call me her songbird and I keep seeing reminders of it." I sat the bird back on the shelf.

A burst of laughter came from the front of the store and I guessed Logan had completed his dare. Then Logan streaked past us, heading toward the restrooms.

I picked up a replica of a gaming token. "You should get her this for sure," I told Sawyer. "It represents this stop the best. Then you can tell her all about Wes's dare to Logan."

Sawyer nodded. "Okay."

I kept studying the shelves, moving down the aisle. At one point, I happened to glance up and see Wes pointing at something and raising his eyebrows at Sawyer who stood next to me. Sawyer shook his head "no" several times. I pretended not to see, turning over more items on the shelves. When Sawyer turned his attention back to the shelves, I looked to where Wes had been pointing. A sprig of some sort of plant hung down from the ceiling above us. It took me a moment to realize it was mistletoe. My heart seemed to stop and then beat double time.

"Amalie," Wes said.

"Wes, don't," Sawyer warned. He didn't know I'd seen it.

"You and Sawyer are standing under mistletoe," Wes continued, undeterred. "If you believe in Christmas at all, you must fulfill the age-old tradition."

Seconds ago, Sawyer had looked annoyed, but when I glanced his way now, he just put on a patient smile. "Don't listen to him."

"Amalie," Wes said. "I dare you."

My heart still wanted to beat out of my chest but I tried to play cool and turned to Sawyer with a shrug. "In the spirit of Christmas?"

"You don't have to," he said.

"I know. You don't either."

"It's not that, it's just . . ."

His crush. I knew why he didn't want to.

"How about on the cheek?" I suggested. I presented my cheek for him.

"Okay."

I don't know what came over me. Maybe it was the dare that Wes had issued, maybe it was some stupid belief that if Sawyer and I kissed, some miracle would occur. But as Sawyer leaned toward me, I turned to face him at the last second. Our lips met. It was a quick peck and he pulled away quickly, *his* cheeks going red for once. Wes cheered.

As far as first kisses went, it wasn't one that was going to change Sawyer's mind about anything. It was too short and unexpected. Plus, he'd pulled away, like I was poison. I forced a laugh, hoping Sawyer wasn't mad at me.

"I'm sorry," I said.

He put his arm around me and kissed me again, on the cheek this time. "Don't be. You're sweet."

Sweet? Great, I'd gotten two kisses today. One real one, and the other the kiss of death.

Wes joined us in our aisle. "My turn?" he asked.

"Sure." I stepped away, leaving Wes and Sawyer under the mistletoe.

Sawyer puckered up for Wes and got punched in the shoulder instead.

Sawyer took the fake coin up to the register, where the man told him no short of twenty times that it wasn't real and was just a novelty and wouldn't work on anything.

I kept browsing and noticed a stack of ninety-nine-cent bookmarks. I looked through the stack, picked one out, along with a bottle of water and a banana, then joined Sawyer at the checkout stand.

"What game are you going to use that coin on first?" I asked Sawyer.

"No," the man said again. "It's not real." He repeated this ten more times and Sawyer narrowed his eyes at me. I bumped his hip with mine. When Sawyer left, I slid the bookmark I'd been hiding onto the counter with my other things and asked for a bag.

As we all walked back to the car, purchases in hand, I couldn't help but think this had been the most fun I'd had in a long time.

DECEMBER 24, 3:30 P.M.

"**W**e have to stop on the Strip," Sawyer said. "Amalie just told me that she's never been."

"You've never been to the Las Vegas Strip?" Heather asked me as she drove.

"No."

"You've been to Italy but not Vegas," Sawyer said shaking his head.

I looked outside. The sun was low in the sky, reflecting off the tall metallic buildings in the distance like some sort of siren call.

"Plus," Wes said. "We can hit up a buffet for dinner."

"We don't have time for a *tourist stop*, children," Heather said. "It's Christmas Eve."

The guys all erupted in various forms of begging.

"We have to at least see the Mirage volcano. It spews real lava!" Logan exclaimed.

"Okay, okay," Heather said at last. "We'll get food at a buffet and stop by *two* hotels. Make them count."

DECEMBER 24, 5:15 P.M.

Our first stop was in front of the Mirage hotel, to see the big volcano. I wasn't sure what the point of it was, but it was large and there were tons of people looking at it. Then we had a cheap buffet dinner at another hotel, and Sawyer kindly paid for me. Now the five of us stood in front of the Bellagio hotel, waiting for the fountains to start. Apparently every fifteen minutes a song played in time with a water show.

"I think we should go to Fremont Street if we only get to stop at two places," Wes said. "It's way cooler than this."

Sawyer held up his hand. "No. Amalie will like this one better."

"Fremont Street isn't even really on the Strip," Heather pointed out. "We're not going there tonight. We still have a six-hour drive home and Mom is already mad that we're so late."

"We can leave," I said.

"No, we're here. This is about to start," Heather said, nodding toward the fountains. "If you like music, you'll like this."

The palm trees that surrounded us were lit up with green-and-white lights and the Bellagio loomed behind the expanse of water. Logan and Wes wandered off to the right, probably settling a dare of some sort, and I glanced over to Sawyer.

"I feel like I've kept you from having fun with your friends the last several days," I told him. "Go ahead. I'm okay here."

"What? Oh, no." Sawyer shook his head. "I've been having fun. I got to hang out with them all weekend."

I was about to respond when the first notes of "O Holy Night" rang out. My mouth clamped shut and my chest expanded. The fountain began spraying—two shoots of water, four, then a wave—all lit up white. My eyes watered as I held them open, unblinking, as the show continued. This was my song. I'd sung it in a Christmas program at the local theater a year ago. I loved this song. It made my heart soar.

All around us, the commotion seemed to pause, and everyone watched and listened.

This was why I loved music. Not because it brought me attention or won me praise or earned me spots in a showcase, but because it could affect emotions. It could speak to a person's soul. It spoke to my soul.

The music built and so did the water, spraying a hundred, two hundred, three hundred feet into the air, probably higher. Goose bumps broke out all along my arms as the music hit its crescendo. And then it was over. The music stopped, the water collapsed back into the pool until it sat like glass, smooth and shiny.

I waited for the encore, but all was still. I was gripping the sleeve of Sawyer's shirt and hadn't even realized it. I let go.

People started walking again, moving around me. My cheeks were wet and I quickly wiped the tears away. Heather no longer stood at my side; I wondered when she had left.

Sawyer still hadn't said anything. Had I completely embarrassed myself? I finally looked at him. "Thank you. That was . . ."

"Heavenly?" he asked.

I laughed. "I was thinking angelic."

"I knew you'd like it."

"I did. I loved it."

"Me too," he said. We were looking at each other now, neither of us making a motion to move.

"We should probably go. It's Christmas Eve," I said.

"Yes, we probably should." He broke eye contact first and looked around for the others. They were up ahead, walking toward the hotel across the street where we'd valeted the car.

"Oh, you forgot to get a gift at this stop," I told Sawyer, secretly happy. Maybe I had distracted him. Maybe he was thinking about me more than her at this point.

"I got something at that place we stopped for the buffet."

"Oh . . . good." Of course he had.

"Hey, guys!" Sawyer called, quickening his pace. "Wait up!"

DECEMBER 25, 12:20 A.M.

It was after midnight when Heather pulled up in front of my house. Christmas morning.

"Thanks so much for letting me crash, everyone," I said, looking around the car. "And, Heather, thank you for driving."

"Of course," Heather replied, turning in her seat. She gave me a warm, genuine smile. "It was great to meet you, Amalie. Come visit me and Sawyer sometime during break. We need a road trip reunion."

"I'd love that," I said, meaning it.

"Maybe Sawyer's crush can join us," Heather added.

I smiled at Sawyer, who stuck his tongue at his sister. "Fingers crossed," I said. I waved good-bye to Wes and Logan, who waved back. Then I hopped out of the car and heard Sawyer follow after me.

"I'll walk you," he said.

"Thanks," I said as I retrieved my backpack.

"You have a key?" he asked.

"I'll go in through the garage." I slung my backpack over one shoulder and walked over to the keypad next to the garage door. I entered the code and the door rolled up noisily. I looked at Sawyer. "Thanks for everything."

"Just don't look up your flight info online and see that your plane beat us."

"Did it?"

"No, of course not." He gave me his famous smile, letting me know that the plane had, in fact, beaten us.

"Either way," I said. "I'm glad I did this."

"Me too."

The sound of a car window rolling down preceded Wes yelling out, "Come on, Sawyer! It's late."

"Good luck," I said. "Are you going to give her the gifts you picked out tomorrow? Or later today, I mean."

Sawyer tilted his head to one side. "Do you think I should? It's Christmas Day. Would I be disrupting family time?"

"I think you should. Just don't spend all day there."

"Okay, good advice."

"I give great advice," I said.

"Merry Christmas, Amalie."

"I got you something, by the way," I added, my heartbeat quickening.

Sawyer frowned. "You got me something? For what?"

"I mean, it's not much but your sister said your family always exchanges gifts on Christmas Eve and I saw this at our Mesquite stop and I don't have a lot of money so I couldn't get you something bigger or better or——"

"Amalie."

I stopped.

He held out his hands. "Are you going to give me my supercheap gift that needed a million disclaimers?"

I pulled the bookmark out of my back pocket and put it in his hands. Sawyer was quiet as he studied it. The bookmark had a picture of a bird on it, which I selfishly hoped would make him think of me every time he used it. Beneath the bird in scrolling script was the Aristophanes quote: *By words the mind is winged.* "Because you like to read . . ."

Before he could say anything, I pulled him into a hug. I closed my eyes, my chin on his shoulder. I wasn't sure if I imagined it or not but it felt like he quickly kissed my temple.

"Merry Christmas," I whispered. Then I rushed into the garage and through the door leading to the house. Once I was inside, I pressed my back against the wall and tried to listen for a shutting car door or an engine driving away. I couldn't hear anything, but when I cracked open the door and looked, the SUV was gone. I let out a pent-up breath and pushed the button to close the garage door. Then I gathered up my courage to face being home.

DECEMBER 25, 12:30 A.M.

The hallway was dark, but I could see lights from the Christmas tree glowing from the living room. That holiday smell I'd come to love assaulted all my senses and I almost cried. But I kept quiet. It would be disorienting and probably not productive to wake my parents up tonight.

I crept up to my brother's room on the second floor. His room was right next to mine. He was only two years younger than I was, and we were close, but apparently not close enough for me to confide in him during the last several months in Italy. I stopped at his doorway, ready to knock, but I changed my mind. I needed sleep.

DECEMBER 25, 8:00 A.M.

The first thing that woke me was the smell of bacon. I knew that my dad, the morning person, was up first to cook us a big breakfast before we filled our stomachs with sugary treats. I sat up in my bed. I hadn't gotten enough sleep but I was immediately awake.

But I waited. I waited until I heard my mom and dad talking in the kitchen. I waited until I heard plates and cups being pulled out of cupboards and my brother's door open and shut. And then I waited another five minutes before I slowly walked down the stairs.

When I arrived in the kitchen my family was eating. My brother saw me first and started choking on orange juice. While my dad was patting his back, my mom noticed me. She dropped her fork.

"Merry Christmas," I said.

"Amalie?" Dad jumped out of his chair and crushed me in a hug. My mom and brother followed.

The happy reunion was soon interrupted with questions. Lots of questions. Some I had answers for, some I didn't. It all came down to the final question. "So you're dropping out?" It was asked by my mom and laced with lots of disappointment.

I thought her tone and her question would make me defensive, would make me unsure of myself again. But I didn't waver this time.

"Yes, Mom." I nodded. "I lost myself there. I was constantly comparing myself to everyone and it was all about the competition and was less and less about the music. I'll get a job, I'll pay back the money you spent on me. But I need to be here now. I need to rediscover everything I love about music. If this would've happened to me in college, it might've thrown me completely off course. But I have time and now I have this experience. I'm going to be okay."

"You're going to be okay?" Mom said.

I nodded, knowing it was true.

Mom burst into tears and hugged me again. "I missed you so much, Amalie. We all missed you so much. I'm sorry I didn't realize what was going on."

"I kept it from you."

"Oh no!" she said, suddenly sounding horrified.

"What?" I asked.

"We mailed your Christmas! Your Christmas is in Italy now. We have nothing for you here."

"Mom." I took her by the shoulders. "You're all here. That's all I want."

Apparently that's exactly what every parent wants to hear because both she and my father hugged me again. Then we talked and caught up while we ate breakfast.

"How did you earn money to get home anyway?" Mom asked while I was scarfing down Dad's delicious food. "I know that's not a cheap plane ticket."

"I gave voice lessons on the side for a couple months with some high school students in Milan," I explained, blushing.

"Amalie, you know that's not allowed," Mom said.

"You're right, I could've gotten kicked out."

She gave a laugh/sigh.

"I know it's super exciting that Amalie is home and everything," Jonathan said, getting to his feet. "But unlike *some* people, I actually have presents to open. So . . ."

My mom smacked my brother's arm playfully. "Jon, we haven't seen your sister in months."

"It's fine, Mom." I laughed. "Let the boy open his presents."

"Oh, what," Jonathan said. "You're super old and mature now?"

"Super."

We went into the living room and sat by the tree. I watched my brother open his gifts and it was nice. Fun, even. I glanced at my phone, not sure exactly what I was looking for. The only people that knew I was home—besides the people in this house—didn't have my number.

Why hadn't I given them my number?

A few hours later, my whole family was in the kitchen; Mom and I were putting wrapping paper in a garbage bag while Dad and Jonathan washed the dishes. Then the doorbell rang.

I looked at my brother and wiggled my eyebrows. "Is that your girlfriend?"

"We broke up."

"What? Why didn't you tell me?"

He shrugged. "I don't know, sis, why didn't you tell me anything?" He smiled at me and went to answer the door.

A moment later, my brother came back in the room and said to me, "You're back one minute and already more popular than me?"

"Someone is here for *me*?" My heart skipped a beat.

"Just someone delivering your luggage."

I punched his arm several times while he laughed. I didn't realize the airlines delivered luggage. And I had no idea they delivered on Christmas Day.

"Make sure you tip them," my mom called as I headed toward the door. "I have some cash in my purse."

I changed direction, grabbed a bill from Mom's wallet, and then rushed to the door. "Sorry, I—" I stopped dead in my tracks. Sawyer stood at the door, my very large suitcase in front of him.

"Hi," he said with a smile. "I thought you might want this." He nodded toward my suitcase. "I see what you meant about your whole life being in here."

"How did you . . . ?"

"I have connections at the airport."

That's right. His dad was a pilot. "Thank you. My mom said to tip you." I held out the cash and he laughed but refused it.

I took the handle of my suitcase and wheeled it into the entry-way, then gestured for him to come inside.

He glanced into the house behind me. "Am I interrupting?"

"No, come in."

He stepped inside and shut the door. "I have something else for you," he said. He pulled a box out from behind him that I hadn't realized he was holding. It was shoebox size and wrapped in blue paper with silver bells on it.

"You didn't have to do that," I said, surprised. "Were you feeling guilty that I got you a ninety-nine-cent gift and you got me nothing?"

"Yes, totally guilty."

"Okay, I'm going to open this and then you're going to tell me how your other gift-giving went today." I led him to the front room off the entryway. The room we barely used because my mom liked to keep it clean for guests that rarely stopped by. I sat on the couch and Sawyer began looking at pictures on the wall.

I carefully peeled back the wrapping, then lifted the lid off the box. Inside were five small, individually wrapped gifts. I unwrapped the first one. It was a snow globe that said *Breckinridge, Colorado*, across the base. Inside was a little skier going down a hill. Had he picked something up at the first stop for me, too? The next present was the silver bird ornament from our second stop. I gasped and looked up. Sawyer was standing there, staring at me, a nervous expression on his face.

I was confused. He'd decided not to give these things to his crush but to me instead? When he didn't say anything, I tentatively opened the next package. It was a pack of gum. I laughed a little. I knew he wouldn't be able to find anything in that seedy motel lobby. I stopped and put the box on the couch next to me.

"Sawyer."

"Amalie." He swallowed hard and started again. "Amalie. I've been thinking about you for the last three years. Please don't find me creepy," he said, quoting Wes from the car.

My thoughts raced. Had Sawyer really been talking about *me* that whole time, or was he just being funny? "But—but you said you'd talked to your crush before and . . ."

"Once," he said. "Last year, at Sarah Farnsworth's graduation party. You were walking down the stairs into the backyard. I was standing in line to get a hamburger. I said, *Hey, I almost wore my yellow sundress too. I'm glad I didn't.* You didn't think I was very funny."

My mind went back to that night, to his face and smile. I had thought he was just friendly with everyone. "I'd forgotten about that. I *did* think you were funny. I was just surprised you were talking to me." I shook my head. "You're right, that was you."

"I know that was me. I see our school interactions were equally as memorable."

"I remember we said hi a couple times in the hallway at school. But at the rental place, you didn't even know my name."

He laughed. "I knew your name, Amalie. You have to give a nervous guy a second to regain his cool. I hadn't seen you in months and suddenly there you were, so chill and beautiful and I wanted you to drive home with us and my brain was working on how I could make that happen."

I was reeling. I hadn't expected this at all. "But when we stood under that mistletoe and I kissed you, you pulled away."

"I didn't want you to kiss me because of a dare."

The dare had just been my excuse. I *wanted* to kiss him. "I'm sorry, I . . ." was overwhelmed and still processing everything.

"You said this gift thing might work," Sawyer said, clasping his hands together. "Is it not working? Too much? I promise I haven't been obsessing over you for three years."

"No, I mean, it's not that. I'm sorry I never . . ."

"Gave me the time of day?"

I laughed. "Yes? I thought you were in a different league."

"I am. A lower one."

"No." Why was I still sitting down? Why was he still standing up? We seemed to both think this thought at the same time because I stood and he took a step toward me and then suddenly we were close. Face to face.

"Will you try again?" I asked.

"What?"

"Start over. Talk to me," I said.

He inched a little closer. "Hey, Amalie. I almost wore my yellow sundress today too. I'm glad I didn't."

I laughed and hit his chest.

He put his hand over mine, holding me there. "Your turn. You're supposed to say something back."

I pushed up onto my toes and kissed him. This time he didn't pull away quickly. He didn't pull away at all. He wrapped his arm around my waist and pulled me closer, deepening the kiss. My hands found his shoulders and traveled to the nape of his neck before he smiled against my mouth and I was forced to pull away.

"You need to open the rest of my gifts," he said.

"I'm kind of enjoying myself right here," I said, but I went back to the couch anyway. This time he sat next to me, his hand on my lower back.

The next gift I knew because I helped him pick it out—the novelty token.

"Next time I'm in Vegas, I'm going to use this," I said.

"It only works in Mesquite," Sawyer said. "At least that's what I think that guy told me."

There was one more gift in the box. The one he'd picked out at our stop in Vegas. The one I was jealous that he had taken the effort to get when I didn't realize it was for me. It was a T-shirt that said, *I found my heart in Vegas.* On the back it said, *It belongs to Elvis.*

"You weren't supposed to look at the back," he said.

I laughed and kissed him again.

"You must've given him a good tip," Jonathan said, walking into the room.

I turned and stood, pulling Sawyer up with me. "Jonathan, Sawyer, Sawyer, my brother, Jonathan."

"I know who you are," Jonathan said to Sawyer. "You're the school president or something, right?"

"Look at that," Sawyer said, turning to me with a grin. "Even your brother knows me more than you did at the beginning of the week."

"Anyway," Jonathan said. "Amalie, Mom is requesting you sing us a Christmas song."

I waited for my throat to tighten at that request. But it didn't. I was home, with family . . . and with Sawyer. I may not have been able to sing to a crowd today or anytime soon, but I knew I could sing here, in this home.

I nodded. "Okay, tell her I'll be right there."

Jonathan left to deliver the message and I turned back to Sawyer.

"So, the last and only time you heard me sing was at a football game three years ago?" I asked.

"Yes."

"Wait . . . is that when . . ."

"I became instantly intrigued with you? Yes."

My cheeks burned. "I now question your ability to discern good music. But come on, it's time to wipe away the sound of horrible speakers from your ears."

Sawyer's face lit up. "I get to hear you sing?"

"Yes. And then tomorrow, I get to hear all your sob stories."

"Again, not sure that is a fair trade-off, but I'm not arguing." I started to drag him into the other room, but he pulled me back toward him and into his arms.

"Yes?" I asked.

"Do you know what I'm grateful for today?"

"What?" I asked, pressing my lips to his.

"Snow, and mistletoe."

WORKING IN
A WINTER WONDERLAND

BY AIMEE FRIEDMAN

"**D**id you ever notice something?" Maxine Silver said into her phone as she strode down Columbus Avenue, passing shops blasting holiday hits at full volume. Each time a bag-laden customer emerged from a store, a snippet of some Christmas song would float out toward Maxine on the crisp December air:

"*Santa baby, slip a sable under the tree for me . . .*"

"*Jingle bell time is a swell time . . .*"

"*All I want for Christmas is . . .*"

"What?" Maxine's best friend, Tara Sullivan, asked on the other end, her mouth full of what Maxine guessed were gingerbread cookies.

"There's a severe shortage of Hanukkah songs," Maxine replied, using her free hand to tug her burgundy scarf higher up her chin. Her teeth chattered as she darted across West 76th Street, a yellow taxicab honking in her wake. She wished she'd remembered to put a hat on over her shaggy-short dark hair when leaving her apartment. Though who could blame her for rushing to escape the embarrassment of her mom and new stepdad, who'd spent the morning frying latkes and inventing pet names for each other? Maxine had been home on winter break for only three days, but she was pretty much ready to go back to college.

"How about, um, the dreidel one?" Tara offered, her voice as sweet as gingerbread itself.

Maxine grinned, picturing Tara standing in the kitchen of her grandparents' house, auburn hair tied back in a ponytail and fair skin flushed with concern. Maxine and Tara had been fused at the hip from the first week of ninth grade on, but since starting their respective freshman years in September—Maxine at Wesleyan, Tara at the University of Chicago—the two girls had only seen each other twice, over Thanksgiving weekend. Tara and her family were spending Christmas in Oregon, so Maxine was all but living for New Year's Eve, when her other half would return to throw her annual gold-and-white-themed party at her apartment.

"You know what I mean," Tara added, and, to Maxine's growing amusement, shifted into slightly off-key singing. There was a reason the girl had been the drummer, and not the lead singer, of The Torn Skirts, their short-lived high school band. "Dreidel, dreidel, dreidel, I made it out of—"

"My point exactly, Tar," Maxine said, passing a row of fresh green trees stacked outside a corner grocery. Stray pine needles crunched beneath the soles of her boots. "'I made it out of *clay*'? Couldn't it at least be a more interesting material?" She rolled her big brown eyes.

Tara's warm laugh bubbled down the line. "Max, I'm sorry. I know you think Hanukkah always gets the shaft."

Maxine sighed and came to a stop in front of a tiny, trendy boutique. "I've gotten used to it after eighteen years. It's like when I was in grade school—somehow, I believed in Santa Claus, but I figured he didn't believe in *me*."

The two girls broke into laughter again, but then Maxine bit her lip. For all her teasing, she *did* get a little bummed around Christmastime. How could she not? What with the mammoth tree glimmering in Rockefeller Center, Starbucks hawking their eggnog lattes, and 90 percent of her friends celebrating else-where, Maxine couldn't help feeling left out of the fun. True, she had once loved Hanukkah—the flickering candles in the meno-rah, the chocolate coins wrapped in bright foil, the plastic top spinning between her fingers—but that was back when her family had still been seminormal.

"New Year's will lift your spirits," Tara assured her. "Have you made any headway toward getting The Dress?"

"I'm drooling over it as we speak," Maxine replied, gazing at the boutique's window display. Amid boughs of holly and twin-kling fairy lights, a mannequin modeled the impossibly perfect dress that Maxine had spied two days ago, and to which she now made regular pilgrimages. Pale gold and floaty, with spaghetti straps and a full, gauzy skirt, The Dress was Maxine's style exactly.

That first day, she'd bounded inside to try it on, fingers tightly crossed; Maxine was so petite ("pixie-esque," Tara liked to call it, while Maxine preferred the more economical "shrimpy") that she often had to buy children's sizes. But, as she'd observed in the fitting room mirror, this very grown-up dress fit her just right. And its color was ideal for Tara's party—to which her best friend was inviting their entire high school class.

Including Heath Barton.

Gorgeous, deep-voiced, cooler-than-thou Heath Barton, whom Maxine had spent the better part of high school lusting after. And even though she'd kissed two boys in college, the thought of Heath, whom Maxine had never really talked to, let alone kissed, still sent tingles down her limbs. She hoped that at Tara's party—emboldened by The Dress—she'd finally have the chance to at least *try* flirting with him.

Then Maxine had glanced at the square tag hanging from the bodice and her stomach had dropped. Were the gods of fashion mocking her? How could a dress so *clearly* designed for her be so out of her price range?

After a whole crazy, fun, stressful semester of buying art history textbooks and late-night pizzas, Maxine had gained a new understanding of the term *flat broke*. The fact that it was Hanukkah—that evening would mark the fourth night of the holiday—was no help. Maxine's family followed the "one big present" rather than the "eight big-ish gifts" philosophy. And since Maxine had already received her gift—a hardcover biography of Johann Sebastian Bach (her mom and stepdad's idea of a "fun read")—it was too late to ask for The Dress. Maxine was criminally behind on her own gift-shopping; that afternoon, she was headed to the Columbus Circle holiday market in search of some cheap-but-respectable presents.

"At this point," Maxine mused aloud to Tara, "the only reasonable thing for me to do would be to get a job." She turned away from the boutique and continued southward on Columbus. The grand white facade, dancing fountains, and brilliantly lit tree of Lincoln Center came into view. Maxine's mom and stepdad were both cellists in the New York Philharmonic, and for one insane instant, Maxine wondered if they could snare her a position there as well—not that her talent for playing bass guitar would get her very far. Maxine *was* passionate about music but, to her mother's chagrin, her tastes ran toward indie bands and garage rock.

"Well, you *could* just look for another dress," Tara was suggesting. Then she paused at the sound of raised voices in the background. "Oh, crap, Max, I have to go. My grandfather needs help fastening our giant inflatable Santa to the roof."

"I'll text you later," Maxine promised.

As she hurried toward the red-and-white-striped booths of the holiday market, Tara's parting advice echoed in her head. Maxine knew her friend had a point. But a stubbornness—a determination—had bloomed in Maxine at the sight of that gold dress. And, as she wandered the crowded aisles of the market, past displays of necklaces, gloves, and fat, scented candles, she wondered if a winter-break job might be the only solution. After all, she reasoned, her home life was driving her nuts, and her social life would be laughable until New Year's. If only she had the slightest idea where to find work. She cast a glance at a nearby stall selling ugly winter hats, as if a HELP WANTED sign might be hanging there.

A sudden, near-arctic wind tore through the market, rattling a display of glass bowls. "Damn, it's *cold!*" someone cried—a tourist, Maxine guessed, who'd been under the mistaken impression that New York City would be balmy on December 17. Shivering, and cursing herself again for forgetting her hat at home, Maxine hurried over to the hat stand. She selected a fuzzy leopard-print number with earflaps. *I'd rather look like a weirdo than die of hypothermia*, she reasoned. She was trying on the hat when she heard a familiar voice behind her.

"Madeline? Madeline Silverman?"

Oh, God. Can it be—

Turning very slowly, her stomach tightening in disbelief, Maxine found herself staring into the bright hazel eyes of Heath Barton.

Yes, Heath Barton. Here he was, standing smack in the middle of the holiday market. His jet-black hair blew across his dark eyebrows and a smile played on his full lips. Maxine noticed that his leather jacket hung open, revealing a black turtleneck and black jeans ripped at the knees. Dazedly, she wondered why he wasn't freezing, until she realized that his own out-of-this-world hotness must have been keeping him nice and toasty. Maxine felt *her* body temperature climbing by the second.

"Madeline," Heath repeated with utter assurance, his square-jawed face now breaking into a wide grin. "From high school. You remember me, right?"

You could say that.

"Oh . . . sure," Maxine said, doing her best imitation of breeziness. She cocked her head to one side, studying him. "Heath . . . Barton, is it?" As he nodded, eyes glinting, she added, "And it's not Madeline, by the way. I'm Maxine. Maxine Silver."

Not that she necessarily expected Heath Barton to remember her name. Back in high school, he'd been the ringleader of the rich-boy slackers and always had some pouty girlfriend—Maxine had nicknamed them "Heathies"—on his arm. Ensconced in her artsy circle of friends, Maxine had outwardly mocked Heath and his ilk but, as Tara well knew, went all jelly-kneed at the sight of him. And there'd been certain moments—right after she'd won first prize in the talent contest for her guitar performance of a Clap Your Hands Say Yeah song, for instance—that Maxine had caught Heath shooting her inquisitive glances that had clearly meant *Hmm . . . maybe sometime*. Maxine had been counting on New Year's, but maybe the time was, well, right now.

Or could have been now, had she not been wearing the leopard-print hat with earflaps.

Just as Maxine's hands were reaching up to remove the unfortunate accessory, Heath stepped forward, eliminating the space between them. "Maxine—that's right," he said, laughing softly. "My bad. I was close though, huh?"

He was certainly getting close. Maxine barely had time to notice that Heath smelled like wood smoke and cider and spice—and that he'd somehow become even hotter since high school—before he plucked the ridiculous hat off her head, his fingers brushing her sideswept bangs. As he set the hat down on the counter beside them, Maxine frantically tried to mash her post-hat hair back into some semblance of place.

"Don't do that." Heath chuckled. "You're ruining the cuteness effect."

Oh no. Maxine wasn't a big blusher, but now she felt an unavoidable warmth stealing up her neck. "I'll keep that in mind," she replied, grinning back at Heath even as her heart drummed like mad. *Tara, wait until I text you now!*

"So catch me up, Maxine Silver," Heath drawled, resting one elbow on the counter as his eyes held hers. "College adventures, crimes, scandals, holiday plans?"

Maxine shrugged, not wanting to spoil the enchanted moment with either generic college stories *or* her litany of winter-break woes. "You know, the usual, I guess," she replied, hoping the conversation would steer its way back to the subject of her supposed cuteness.

"I'm *stoked* to be out of New Haven," Heath confessed with a world-weary sigh, running a hand through his floppy hair. "There's nothing like winter in the city—chilling with my boys, helping out my dad at his store—" Heath paused meaningfully, and raised an eyebrow at Maxine. "Oh—I'm not sure if you know who my dad—I mean—" He ducked his head.

Maxine nodded. "I know," she whispered. *Everyone* knew who Heath's father was: Cecil Barton III, owner of Barton's, the sumptuous jewel box of a department store on Fifth Avenue. Maxine remembered the buzz Mr. Barton, in his bow tie and bowler hat, had created at their graduation alongside Heath's mother, who was an equally famous—and stunning—Japanese former supermodel.

"I'm actually here for my dad today," Heath was saying. "Doing market research—to check out the competition and all." With a slight air of distaste, he gestured to the packed stalls around them. "Technically I'm supposed to be on my lunch break but we're so swamped at the store that I've got to mix business with pleasure." Maxine was forcing herself not to fixate on the word *pleasure* coming out of Heath's mouth when he rolled his long-lashed eyes and went on. "It's madness over there—one of our salespeople quit this morning so the manager wasn't giving me a moment's rest. I was all like, 'Mr. Perry, can I at least grab a latte?' and he was like—"

"Wait." The word had escaped Maxine's lips almost without her realizing it. *Swamped at the store. Salesperson quit.* She felt inspiration flood through her body, making her skin prickle and her breath catch. She found she couldn't move. "There's—there's an opening at Barton's?" she asked. Furiously, her mind fought to process this incredible piece of information. An opening, just when she most needed a job? An opening at the very place where *Heath Barton himself was working*?

It was a freaking Hanukkah miracle.

"Uh-huh," Heath said distractedly, reaching into his jacket pocket and pulling out his phone. Then he lifted his head and met Maxine's gaze, which she knew must have been wild-eyed and borderline manic. She tried to compose her features into a mask of glamorous sophistication, but then Heath's own eyes widened, and his lips parted. "Maxine, are *you* interested?" he murmured. He tilted his head to one side, clearly sizing her up— though for what, Maxine wasn't sure. Then Heath spoke again, sending all the blood rushing to her face.

"You'd be perfect" was what Heath Barton said. "Perfect for the position."

The flattery roared in Maxine's ears, half drowning out the rest of what Heath was saying—something about how she should go see Mr. Perry now if she was seriously interested, because those types of positions were usually snatched up right away.

"I can totally stop by Barton's now," Maxine exclaimed. She almost burst into laughter over her unexpectedly sweet fortune. "Want to walk back with me?" she added casually, as if the thought of an afternoon stroll with Heath wasn't making her belly flip over.

"I'd love to, Maxine," Heath replied, knitting his brows together, while Maxine decided that she could never tire of hearing her name in his deep voice. "Only I still need to run a couple of errands for my dad. But hey—" He took another step closer, rested a hand on the sleeve of her corduroy jacket, and gave her arm a small squeeze. "Good luck, okay? If you get the position, maybe I'll see you at the store tomorrow?"

Forget *maybe*. Maxine Silver was going for the gold.

❊   ❊   ❊

She could still feel the warmth of Heath's hand on her arm moments later, as she flew down Central Park South, passing the Essex House and the Plaza, unable to stop grinning. Working at Barton's! Visions of free makeup, marked-down jeans, and, most tantalizing of all, daily doses of Heath Barton danced in her head. Maybe while she was folding cashmere sweaters, Heath would swing by and suggest they mix business and pleasure *together*. Maxine giggled out loud at the thought, prompting a curious glance from a family waiting in line for a horse-and-carriage ride. Normally Maxine would have ignored them, but she was so suffused with goodwill that she waved a mittened hand at the pigtailed little girl.

Her scarf streaming behind her like a victory flag, Maxine rounded onto Fifth Avenue, where a giant, sparkling white snowflake hung overhead, as it did every holiday season. Panting and a little sweaty from her impromptu workout, Maxine paused on the corner of 58th Street and stared up at the snowflake as if it were her personal good-luck pendant. *Please, please let me get the job*, she prayed silently.

Then she pulled her compact out of her bag and did a scan of her flushed face. Her hands unsteady, she brushed the powder puff over her upturned nose and across her red cheeks, and made one last attempt at flattening her unruly hair. She was as ready as she'd ever be. *You can rock this*, she told herself, imagining the pep talk Tara would have given her had she been there. Tossing her head back, Maxine whirled around and pulled open the heavy double doors of Barton's.

Ah.

Classical music filtered down past the soft white globes dangling from the arched ceiling. The walls were painted a creamy color, except for the farthest one, which was dominated by a black-and-pink mural of a high-heeled woman walking a poodle in London. That poodle, Maxine knew, was Barton's logo—the image that appeared on every shopping bag, gift box, and advertisement. It was a little bizarre to associate the poodle with Heath Barton, and Maxine pressed her lips together to keep from snorting. *Remain elegant*, she told herself, drifting inside.

Maxine hadn't been to Barton's in years, and now she breathed in everything anew. A long glass perfume counter, dotted with crimson poinsettias, rippled through the center of the store like a clear river. Behind the counter, chic salespeople murmured to one another as they sprayed customers' wrists with designer scents. *I could work there*, Maxine realized. But then there was the makeup counter across the store, where white-jacketed men and women wielded gold-plated eyebrow pencils. Maxine figured she could be a quick study when it came to doing makeovers.

And then, toward the back of the store, the luckiest of salespeople flitted through racks of clothes like fairies in a colorful forest. Sighing with appreciation, Maxine let her fingers dance over velvet jackets, silky dresses, and fuzzy cardigans. As she advanced toward the back office, where Heath had told her to go, she passed two winding staircases, and noticed that one led down to a cavernous space devoted solely to shoes. *And* that's *where I want to be stationed*, Maxine decided with a smile, reaching the slightly ajar door to the manager's office.

Maxine knocked once and then pushed the door all the way open to reveal a skinny young man with a goatee, wearing a button-down shirt, necktie, and burgundy-framed glasses. He was sitting at a cluttered desk, frantically typing something on a laptop in between taking bites of a Krispy Kreme doughnut. A jar full of candy canes sat on the windowsill, the only nod to the season. This image didn't quite jibe with Barton's high fashion vibe, but Maxine didn't care—she'd made it to the inner sanctum.

"Mr. Perry?" Maxine ventured, and the man glanced up from his laptop, lifting his glasses to his forehead and squinting at Maxine.

"You lost, honey?" he asked. "The fitting rooms are downstairs, with the shoes—"

"Mr. Perry, Heath Barton told me to come see you," Maxine interjected hurriedly. She felt a small glow of pride at being able to toss that powerful name around.

89

But to Maxine's surprise, Mr. Perry only sighed and rubbed at his eyes. "Did he? Enlighten me. What could the ever-helpful young heir have sent you here for?" Then Mr. Perry shook his head and feigned a look of horror. "But *shhh*. We can't be caught talking like that about *the boss's son*." As he spoke, Mr. Perry pointed over his shoulder to a framed painting on the wall of Cecil Barton III himself, who gazed down imperiously in his ever-present bow tie and bowler hat. "I think the old man's bugged the office, to tell you the truth."

Despite herself, Maxine felt her lips twitch. She couldn't help but like Mr. Perry.

"Well," Maxine began, casting a look at the paperwork on Mr. Perry's desk and realizing with a sinking sensation that she should have brought her resume. And references. And—oh, God—how could she have been so *stupid*, dashing over here on a whim? Suddenly Maxine understood how glaringly unprepared she was for this job. She had no experience in retail. She was filled with the urge to turn around and walk out as surely as she'd come in. They'd never take her at Barton's.

"Yeah?" Mr. Perry prompted, still squinting at Maxine as if she were an oversized insect who'd fluttered her way into his office.

Figuring she had nothing to lose, Maxine took a deep breath and plunged ahead. "Heath told me that there was an opening for a salesperson, and that he thought I'd be—"

Mr. Perry's jaw dropped and he shifted his glasses back into place, staring at Maxine. "Perfect," he finished for her, and

Maxine felt a chill race down her spine. *The exact same word Heath had used.* "God, yes," Mr. Perry went on, his face lighting up with wonder. "Maybe that kid *isn't* totally useless. Come in, come in—what's your name?" Mr. Perry asked, motioning for Maxine to take a seat in the chair across from him.

In a matter of minutes, to Maxine's amazement, everything was squared away: Mr. Perry, all excitement, informed her of the pay (which was higher than Maxine had expected) and told her that the position was a temporary one, only running until December 24. Maxine took this as good news, since she'd be returning to college in January. After she had eagerly agreed to Mr. Perry's request that she start tomorrow at nine A.M. sharp, the manager ceremoniously handed her a few forms to fill out, and that was that.

"You just need to try on your costume, and then we'll be set," Mr. Perry said, getting to his feet and heading toward the wardrobe in the corner. "I'm sure it will fit fine, but it might need to be taken in here and there."

Maxine, who had been hastily signing her name on a dotted line, glanced up, startled. *Costume?* Mr. Perry must have been referring to the white-jacketed uniform Maxine had seen on the makeup people. She was about to ask him if she could get a lesson in applying foundation when Mr. Perry turned toward her with a dramatic "Voilà!"

But Mr. Perry wasn't holding up a starched white jacket.

No.

He was holding up a bright-green long-sleeved leotard, a red cotton drawstring miniskirt, green-and-white-striped tights, and a plastic headband with enormous, pointy, green plastic ears on either end.

It was an elf costume.

Maxine's stomach lurched. "Um—I—I think—" *I think there's been a mistake*, she wanted to say, but she was too stunned to force the words from her throat.

"You can change in there," Mr. Perry told her. He gestured to an adjoining room, oblivious to the color rapidly draining from Maxine's face. "It's the employee dressing room."

"But—" Maxine's voice came out raspy, and she coughed. "Where am I supposed to *wear* that?" she whispered hoarsely. Maybe trying on the costume was part of some weird Barton's initiation ceremony. She cast a glance up at Cecil Barton III, who glared back at her.

Mr. Perry furrowed his brow. "Upstairs. In our Christmas Corner? Didn't Heath tell you? Our second floor is devoted to all things Christmas this time of year. That's why, when our only elf quit on us, we needed a replacement so badly."

Maxine felt the pen slip out from between her fingers. It fell to the floor with a clatter.

You have got to be kidding me.

Maxine glanced down at her signature on the paper, her body going numb. Getting to her feet and running from the office seemed like the best possible plan, but Maxine also knew that would be the cowardly way out. Heath had gone to the trouble of telling her about this position, Mr. Perry seemed so hopeful to have her on board, *and* she'd already signed all the forms . . . The least she could do was try on the stupid costume. The get-up probably wouldn't even fit, or it would look so howlingly awful on her that Mr. Perry would assign her to some other post in the store.

Feeling as if she were moving through molasses, Maxine walked over to Mr. Perry to accept the clothes. Maxine started toward the dressing room, when, as if from a great distance, she heard the manager speak again.

"We can't forget the shoes," he said, holding out a pair of green satin slip-ons with toes that curled up at the tips. "Without them, the outfit doesn't really work, you know?"

Inside the cramped changing room, as she stripped off her jeans and hoodie, Maxine had a flashback to the fitting room where she'd tried on The Dress. Only now she wasn't wriggling into a luscious gold confection, but a pair of thick tights and a stretchy, itchy leotard. *Kill me.* She was careful not to face the mirror, even when she adjusted the faux ears over her own, securing them in place with the plastic headband that went over her hair. Next came the shoes, into which Maxine's size-five feet slid with surprising ease. Right as she was bracing herself to turn and survey the damage, Mr. Perry knocked.

"Ready?" he asked and Maxine opened the door for him. "Oh, wow," he gasped, his eyes growing round behind his glasses. "Look at *you!*"

Cringing, Maxine turned to face her reflection—and her heart sank. Because, in that instant, she understood why everyone had thought her so "perfect" for the job. She *looked* like an elf, the pointy ears emphasizing her delicate features and close-cropped hair, the striped tights and upturned shoes somehow working on her tiny frame. As much as it pained Maxine to admit it, the entire costume fit as if it had been made specifically for her.

And, glancing at Mr. Perry's rapt expression, Maxine knew there was no way she could turn and run out of his office now. She was in too deep. Besides, she reminded herself, she *did* need a job. And maybe she wouldn't have to wear the elf costume *constantly*. Maybe she could change out of it for her lunch breaks, and hide from Heath the rest of the time.

Facing her new boss, Maxine held her breath and gave Mr. Perry a quick nod.

Yes, sir, I'd love to be subjected to public humiliation.

Mr. Perry smiled and extended a hand toward her, message clearly received. "Welcome to Barton's," he said. "And merry Christmas!"

❄ ❄ ❄

"Happy Hanukkah!" Maxine heard her stepdad, Scott Levy, call as she dragged herself into her apartment that evening. The strains of her mother's cello drifted toward her, along with the rich scent of potato pancakes. Maxine's stomach growled; after the insane events of that afternoon, she was mentally and physically drained.

"Happy happy," Maxine muttered in response, kicking off her boots in the foyer. Her mind still on elves, Mr. Perry, and Heath Barton, she headed into the cozy living room, where her mother sat on a low stool, her curly black hair falling into her eyes as she practiced. Scott's own cello was propped up in the corner, beside the oak bookshelves. Scott himself stood at the dining room table, holding a box of Hanukkah candles in one hand. The family's menorah was perched before him with four candles in place, waiting to be lit.

"Why so glum, Max?" Scott inquired, shooting Maxine a boy-ish grin. It wasn't all that difficult for Maxine's stepdad to look boyish—because he was only twenty-nine years old. As in: eleven years older than Maxine, and many more years younger than Maxine's mother. Scott's age made it all the harder for Maxine to remotely see him as anything *parental*.

"I got a job today," Maxine replied over the cello music, reaching for the plate of latkes on the table. "At a department store." For obvious reasons, she didn't feel like elaborating. She could just imagine Scott doing some lame Will-Ferrell-in-*Elf* impersonation. Studying the menorah and the latkes before her, Maxine couldn't quite believe that in a matter of hours she'd be dressed as one of Santa's helpers and selling Christmas tree orna-ments. Talk about culture shock.

"Mazel tov, Max—that's so cool!" Scott exclaimed, his expression bright and earnest. As always, Maxine felt a pinch of guilt for how she treated Scott—he wasn't a bad guy, but she wished he'd stop trying so hard to be her BFF. At the same time, she didn't want him playing the Dad role, either. Maxine already had a father—who, at the moment, just happened to be living on a kibbutz in Israel. That was where he'd run off to three years ago, when he'd decided that being an attorney was destroying his hippie soul.

"What's this about a job?" Maxine's mother called. She stopped playing and hurried over to the table, the bell sleeves of her floaty black dress swinging back and forth. Rather than wait for Maxine's response, she snuggled up to Scott, sliding her arms around his neck and running her fingers through his light-brown hair. "I missed you, Shmoopy," she whispered.

I'm going to be ill, Maxine thought, dropping her half-eaten latke on a napkin. "You missed him from all the way across the room?" she couldn't help but ask, rolling her eyes.

"Maxine, please drop the sarcasm for one night," her mother snapped, giving Maxine a quick, dismissive glance before turning her attention back to Shmoopy.

Maxine managed to keep the rest of her comments to herself as Scott lit the menorah and recited the Hebrew blessing. Although it was her second Hanukkah with Scott there, Maxine didn't think she'd *ever* get used to seeing him in the role that had once been her father's. As the small, teardrop-shaped flames wavered on the candles and Maxine half-heartedly joined in singing "Rock of Ages," her throat tightened. Not just because she was feeling nostalgic for Hanukkahs past, but because, watching her mom and Scott hold hands, she felt a pang of longing. Suddenly Maxine wished she were spending this sweet, warm holiday not with her mom and stepdad—or even her real dad—but with someone sweet and warm, an adorable guy who would actually care about the job she'd gotten that day, and want to hold her hand while singing.

Heath. Glancing down, Maxine smiled to herself as anticipation rippled through her. Despite her ten thousand qualms about working in the Christmas Corner, the plain fact remained: She'd be seeing Heath Barton tomorrow—and every single day for the next week. And that, Maxine hoped, might just be worth the epic mortification of those pointy ears.

❆ ❆ ❆

At nine twenty the next morning, Maxine, in all her elfin glory, anxiously ascended the winding staircase to Barton's Christmas Corner. She was about to meet her direct supervisor, Sandy Teasdale, whom Mr. Perry had explained would be waiting for Maxine upstairs. When Maxine had come to his office to pick up her costume, the manager had told her that though she needed to be there early for her first day, the other salespeople didn't show up until nine thirty because the store opened to the public at ten. Placing one curly-toed foot on the second-floor landing, Maxine wondered when Heath got in, and her heart leaped.

"Elf?" a brusque voice demanded, and Maxine gave a start, glancing up.

In the middle of a red-and-green-painted space crammed to the hilt with Christmas stockings, reindeer figurines, life-size candy canes, and countless other sparkly objects, stood a tall, unsmiling woman in her mid-forties. She wore a high-necked green tweed suit and green pumps, and her wavy red hair tumbled out from beneath a velvet Santa hat. She was holding a clipboard and scowling at Maxine.

"Sandy?" Maxine guessed.

Sandy didn't look up from her clipboard as she fired off a stern monologue. "As a Christmas Corner employee, you are responsible for assisting our customers in their quest for the perfect Christmas-oriented item, be it a handmade Advent calendar, a ruby Rudolph nose, or a blown-glass angel. Apart from a half-hour lunch break, you must constantly be on hand to offer purchasing advice, wrap gifts, and spread holiday cheer. Do I make myself clear?"

Maxine gulped. "Um, could you clarify the 'holiday cheer' part?" she asked.

Sandy nodded briskly. "Once a day, whenever I give the signal, you and the other Christmas Corner employees will gather over there"—she pointed toward a spot near a display of chocolate snowmen—"and break into a song of my choosing." Sandy cleared her throat and consulted the clipboard. "Today's is 'Winter Wonderland.'"

Maxine wondered if she was being punished for a crime committed in a former life. "The other employees?" she repeated, since it was easier to focus on that than the song issue. Until now, Maxine hadn't given much thought to the possibility of costumed coworkers who would share in her misery.

Sandy lifted her chin and pointed over Maxine's shoulder. "Here they come now."

Turning around, Maxine watched with mingled trepidation and curiosity as two guys and a girl—all about her age—trooped over. The girl was gorgeous, with dark-brown skin, a long neck, and a straight, graceful carriage. She wore her curly brown hair pinned up in a bun, upon which rested a silver tiara. With a stab of jealousy, Maxine took in the rest of her costume: a white top with wings attached to the back, and a pale pink tutu. Maxine wished *she'd* been lucky enough to snag the pretty ballet costume. Then she turned her attention to the guys. One of them, who had straight blond hair and freckles, wore a scarlet military-style suit complete with epaulets and gold buttons, and carried a black box-shaped hat under his arm. At his side was a short, pale guy with shoulder-length brown hair. He wore a red jogging suit and black boots, and a Santa hat swung casually from his hand.

"Meet the Sugarplum Fairy, the Nutcracker Prince, and Santa Claus," Sandy told Maxine in her flat, hard monotone. Pursing her lips at Santa Claus, she added, "Where on earth is your beard?"

Santa's mouth dropped open and his dreamy eyes widened. "Oh, dude. I knew I forgot *something*." Scratching his head, he turned and headed back downstairs as Maxine watched him, fighting the urge to crack up.

"Nutcracker, please fill Elf in on the rest," Sandy was saying. "I need to set up the register before we open."

Feeling new-girl-at-school-ish, Maxine turned to face her two colleagues, and raised her eyebrows at them, twisting her hands behind her back.

Nutcracker grinned, his blue-gray eyes dancing. "The first thing I should tell you is that, believe it or not, we all have real names. This is Claudette Lambert," he explained, gesturing to the Fairy, who gave Maxine a welcoming smile. "Santa's Daniel Matheson, and I'm Avery Prince."

"Prince?" Maxine felt a wry smile tug on her lips. "For real? So you just swapped 'Avery' for 'Nutcracker' to get this job?" Maxine hoped she wasn't offending the guy; her mom often chided her about not thinking before she spoke.

But Nutcracker—or, rather, Avery—only shook his head, still smiling. "One of those lucky coincidences, I guess," he replied cheerily.

Oh God. Maxine groaned inwardly. Mr. Blond Sunshine was clearly lacking in the humor department.

When Santa/Daniel returned, hat cockeyed on his head and frothy white beard covering his chin, Maxine hurriedly intro-duced herself to the trio, accepting the fact that, like it or not, she was one of them now.

Then Avery gave her another aw-shucks smile. "Let me show you our wrapping station," he said, his voice brimming with enthusiasm. As Maxine reluctantly turned to follow him, her curly-toed slipper made contact with a stack of yule logs, and she tripped, stumbling forward a few paces. *Great*. Not like Claudette's prima-ballerina presence wasn't already making her feel like the biggest klutz alive. At least Heath wasn't around to witness her smooth moves.

"Easy there, Ms. Elf," Daniel said, taking hold of Maxine's shoulder. "You cool?" Maxine couldn't make out Daniel's mouth behind the beard but his brown eyes were smiling, and she smiled back. She suspected that Slacker Santa's chill vibe might make her time at the Christmas Corner slightly more bearable.

"I'm grand," Maxine replied. "I mean, who doesn't enjoy strolling in elf shoes?" Daniel and Claudette glanced at each other, chuckling.

"Well, our last elf, for one," Avery chimed in with predictable earnestness. He motioned for Maxine to join him at a counter that was strewn with tubes of red, gold, and green wrapping paper.

"Yeah, why *did* she quit?" Maxine asked, feeling a prickle of intrigue. "Or was it death by embarrassment?"

Claudette shook her head. "She got a job at the fry station at Burger Heaven."

Maxine nodded, her worst fears confirmed. So dunking your gloved hands into vats of hot oil was preferable to working the elf gig at Barton's.

Maxine walked—carefully—over to Avery at the gift wrap counter.

"Wrapping gifts, in my humble opinion, is the second-best part of our job," Avery was saying, resting his boxy hat on the counter. "People are so grateful, when all you've really done is slap on some paper and Scotch tape——"

"Um, sorry," Maxine cut in, annoyed beyond belief by Avery's ode to gift wrapping. "There's a *first* best part to our job? Like what, leaving for the day?"

Avery glanced at Maxine, furrowing his brow. "Wow. Are you always this cynical?" he asked, his tone matter-of-fact.

Maxine rolled her eyes. She was a native New Yorker, for God's sake——she was allowed a little cynicism now and then. Meanwhile, she'd bet anything that Nutcracker Prince wasn't from here. He'd probably grown up in a ranch house, called his dad "Pop," and got *really* into Christmas.

"My favorite part is the kids," Avery was saying, fastening his black hat on over his blond head. "You'll see——they get so psyched about the smallest things and——"

"I can imagine," Maxine said, picturing a screaming brood of five-year-olds fighting over the display of gourmet candy apples.

On cue, she heard a cacophony of excited voices streaming up the staircase, along with a boy whining, "Mom, can I get a toy sleigh this year, please, can I, can I?" Glancing at the clock above the cash register, Maxine's stomach sank. It was ten o'clock. Barton's was open for business. No turning back now.

"Well, here we go," Avery said, tipping the brim of his soldier's hat to Maxine and flashing her a grin. "Good luck, Maxine."

As Avery marched off, Maxine scanned the faces of the people swarming upstairs, hoping to catch sight of her crush's messy black hair and sly smile. But Heath was nowhere to be seen, and soon the entire space was so flooded with customers that Maxine had no time to dwell on finding him.

Haggard-looking parents, grandparents, and nannies—with grabby toddlers in tow—descended upon Maxine at once. *Where are the hand-painted Belgian eggnog ladles? Is that Christmas tree for sale? Do you carry faux-fur stockings?* "Um, it's my first day," Maxine replied, breaking out in a sweat and searching for some colleague to come to her aid. But Sandy was at the register, Claudette was pirouetting around the snow globe display, Daniel was half dozing behind the gift wrap counter, and Avery was good-naturedly posing for a photo with a pack of little boys. Maxine tried to answer the storm of questions as they came, but she was distracted by countless elbows in her ribs and a random baby yanking on her elf ears each time he passed by in his father's arms. The fact that she made it through the morning without getting trampled seemed a small triumph.

Lunch, Maxine learned, consisted of egg salad sandwiches provided by Sandy, and Maxine wolfed hers down while sitting alone on a carton in the back storage room. So much for changing out of her elf costume and meeting Heath; the half hour barely allowed her time to finish chewing her food and to tug up her striped tights, which were bunching around the knees.

By three o'clock, the mad rush had trickled down enough for Maxine to do a quick spin around the Corner, mentally taking note of where the Belgian eggnog ladles and various other items were kept. When an elderly woman cradling a Chihuahua demanded that Maxine find her the priciest tree ornament in the shop, Maxine produced a Swarovski-crystal-encrusted star in five seconds flat, and couldn't help feeling a flush of pride. But just as Maxine was handing over the ornament, she heard Sandy calling her and the others over to the chocolate snowmen display.

The singing portion of the afternoon, Maxine realized. Dread gripped her as she watched Sandy set up speakers. Daniel, Avery, and Claudette gathered in a semicircle. Her palms clammy, Maxine headed over, positioned herself between Avery and Claudette, and accepted the sheet of lyrics from Sandy. As the opening chords of "Winter Wonderland" filled the Christmas Corner, Sandy stood before her four employees and held her arms out on either side like a conductor. Maxine wondered how her mom and stepdad, the music snobs, would react to this moment. Some customers reacted by stopping and staring, while others continued milling about, indifferent to or perhaps familiar with this act of lunacy.

"One, two, three . . . Sleigh bells ring!" Sandy sang at the top of her lungs, swooping her arms in and out.

"Are you listening?" Claudette, Avery, and Daniel chimed right in, singing in loud unison over the backup track pouring out of the speakers. "In the lane, snow is glistening . . ."

Maxine remained frozen in horror.

Avery lightly nudged her with his elbow, indicating that she should add her voice to the chorus, and Maxine felt a spark of irritation. *What a kiss-up*, she thought, glancing over at him; true to form, he was singing with abandon, not even referring to the lyrics in his hand. Meanwhile Claudette was trilling in a beautiful soprano, practically auditioning for the opera. But thankfully Daniel was stumbling over the words—"in the snowman we can build a meadow"—and when Maxine caught his eye, he made a face. Feeling a little better, Maxine started singing along, realizing she was familiar with the lyrics. After all, Christmas music played on a near-constant loop inside every store and taxicab the minute Thanksgiving ended; over the years, something had clearly sunken in.

Out in the crowd, a nanny and her young charge joined in the singing, and someone else cheered. Maxine felt a laugh building in her. Somehow the moment was so ludicrous that it was almost . . . fun. She'd forgotten the pure pleasure that came with singing; sometimes it didn't matter what the music was. As long as no one she actually *knew* was watching—

Oh no.

Maxine was belting out the part about your nose getting a "chilling" when she spotted a face in the crowd that made her voice catch. Heath Barton was standing a few feet away, a Starbucks venti cup in one hand and sunglasses hiding his hazel eyes. As the corner of his mouth lifted in a teasing grin, he raised his cup toward Maxine in greeting, and her face turned so hot she was sure it matched Daniel's Santa suit.

"Congrats," Heath said, strolling over to Maxine a few minutes later, once all the customers had dutifully applauded.

"You mean on surviving that?" Maxine asked, out of breath. Heath's nearness was making her pulse accelerate. She brushed her sweaty bangs off her forehead, wondering if she could duck behind the Christmas tree and pull herself together. Her elf ears felt like they might be askew.

"On getting the job, silly," Heath replied, taking a sip from his cup. "Having a good morning so far?"

Maxine blinked up at him in confusion. "Heath, it's like three thirty."

"Is it?" Heath removed his shades and checked his phone. "Oh, man, whenever I wake up at noon, it throws my whole day off." He glanced over as Claudette, Avery, and Daniel passed by. "'Sup, Claudette?" he called. "Heard you got the lead in *Swan Lake*. Nice." He shot her a winning smile and then looked back at Maxine. "She's a dancer at Juilliard," he explained, lowering his voice.

Of course, Maxine thought, glancing at Claudette, who returned Heath's smile and said something to Avery and Daniel. Maxine noticed that all three of them were watching her and Heath with interest. She knew her coworkers must have been curious about Maxine's connection to Barton's heir.

"I need to jet—I'm having lunch with my dad's accountant," Heath was saying, touching Maxine's shoulder to get her attention. "Lately I've been more involved with the business side of the store," he added, and motioned to the cash register. "It all comes down to bills, bills, bills in the end. You know what I mean?"

"I guess," Maxine replied, thinking that actually it all came down to Heath's hand on her shoulder right then.

"Speaking of," Heath went on, sliding his hand from Maxine's shoulder down to her arm, making her stomach jump. "We should do lunch sometime."

Maxine nodded, trying to keep a poker face. "But I've only got half an hour," she explained. "Maybe instead we could—" She paused, wondering if it would be too forward to ask about night-time plans. She pictured herself and Heath, hands linked, strolling along Fifth Avenue and gazing into the glowing window displays as snow drifted down on them. They would stop to watch the ice skaters at Rockefeller Center and . . .

"No worries," Heath said, dropping his voice to a whisper. "I'll talk to Mr. Perry, pull some strings to get you more free time." He gave her a conspiratorial wink, slowly removed his hand from her arm, and turned to go while Maxine watched him, melting. "And, hey, Maxine?" Heath added, glancing back at her before he descended the staircase. "You make some elf."

Before Sandy could scold her for standing around doing nothing, Maxine hurried toward the gift wrap counter, her heart racing. She was dying to text Tara to confer about whether or not *You make some elf* was code for *I love you*.

❄   ❄   ❄

That week at Barton's, Heath gave Maxine endless fodder for texts, since he visited the Christmas Corner daily, always delivering a flirtatious remark ("Hot tights, Silver"), and, once, a kiss on the cheek. The kiss came after a disastrous group rendition of "Hark! the Herald Angels Sing," so when Heath unexpectedly leaned close, whispered, "Nice work," and pressed his warm lips to Maxine's skin, it felt like a reward. Maxine took a step back and grinned up at him. Daniel, Claudette, and Avery were lingering nearby, but Maxine was barely aware of her coworkers, or the rest of the Christmas Corner crush around her.

"I'm sorry I haven't made good on that lunch date," Heath said, his hand lightly brushing the spot he had kissed as he moved a strand of hair off Maxine's face. "I promise I'll talk to Mr. Perry once my schedule has calmed down a little."

"You do that," Maxine replied, although she wasn't sure what exactly was keeping him so busy. After only a few days at Barton's, she'd realized that Heath didn't technically "work"—he floated, drifting from one part of the store to the other, coming and going at odd hours to conduct "market research," and chatting up the girls who worked at the perfume counter to "assess employee satisfaction." But Maxine couldn't quibble; their flirtations by the Christmas tree, however brief, were still delicious oases in the midst of all those giant candy canes and shrieking children.

Though it turned out that Heath Barton wasn't the only bright spot in her existence as an elf. Those shrieking children, for instance, could actually be pretty darn cute. On her second day, Maxine had a bonding moment with a wide-eyed little girl who tugged on her hand and asked if she really worked in Santa's toy shop. "Yes, and I'll make some extras for you this year!" Maxine had replied, startled by the sweetness of her own response. As the girl's face lit up, Maxine wondered if Avery hadn't been so off base after all. And though Maxine wasn't in love with gift wrapping just yet, helping frantic customers *could* be weirdly rewarding. Once she'd familiarized herself with the layout of the store, Maxine became something of an expert at digging up obscure items—from extra-large Santa suits to the last remaining Prancer figurine—and presenting them to people who were near tears. "Ask Maxine" became a catchphrase among her coworkers, and hearing those words gave Maxine a warm rush of pride.

Maxine's coworkers had turned out to be another not-so-bad aspect of the job. Despite her predilection for doing *tour jetés* across the Christmas Corner, Claudette was as sweet as her job title promised; during lunch, she and Maxine sometimes snuck downstairs to *ooh* and *ahh* over new clothing shipments. Even Avery's boundless enthusiasm, which had irked Maxine from the start, could be refreshing at times, especially when he volunteered to take over cleanup duty at the end of a long, grueling day. And Daniel's *whatever-dude* philosophy proved as comforting as Maxine had predicted, though his tendency to take naps under the Christmas tree got annoying.

Mostly, though, Maxine was glad to have compatriots under Sandy's tyrannical rule. One sleet-drenched morning, when Sandy was stuck in traffic and running late, Avery offered to head out to the corner café and pick up mochas for everyone.

With some time to kill before ten, the foursome gathered around the register with their drinks and swapped stories about what had brought them to Barton's.

"Houston," Claudette sighed in her tinkly voice, cupping her chin in her hands and gazing off into the distance. "I just need to afford a plane ticket home to Houston for Christmas, and then everything will be okay."

"How so?" Maxine asked, sipping her mocha. As usual, Daniel and Avery were staring at Claudette in utter, silent devotion, as if every word she breathed were gospel.

Claudette lifted her shoulders, her wings fluttering behind her. "Lance," she explained. "My love. He's there, waiting for me. It's not really Christmas if we're not together."

Maxine fought the urge to roll her eyes while Daniel and Avery both looked crestfallen at this news.

"I'm feeling you on the plane ticket front," Daniel spoke up, fiddling with his Santa beard. "Otherwise, I'll need to hitch a ride to San Diego. My parents will—no joke—assassinate me if I'm not home for Christmas. My family's nuts."

Maxine nodded, thinking that she could relate to *that*. Meanwhile, Avery asked Daniel if that was why he moved out east in the first place.

"Not really," Daniel replied, shifting his beard back into place. "I'm a film student at The New School. I took this job because I want to make a documentary about department-store

Santas. It's gonna be, like, Oscar-worthy. When I get around to doing it, that is."

"Cool," Avery replied. Glancing at Maxine, he bit his lower lip and a dimple appeared in his left cheek. Maxine wondered if, like her, he was trying not to laugh. It was odd to share a moment of connection with Avery, but then Maxine brushed the feeling aside. He may have been good-looking—in a generic, vanilla sort of way—but he was *so* not someone Maxine would even be friends with outside this job.

"What about you?" Maxine asked Avery, breaking their gaze and focusing on her mocha. "Why Barton's?"

"I'm studying acting at Tisch—you know, New York University?" Avery explained. "I figured this job would be good practice for an aspiring actor. And I'm from Illinois, so—"

"Illinois?" Maxine repeated, grinning, and Avery nodded, taking a sip of his mocha. *Bingo!* she thought. Her Midwesterner radar never failed her.

Next it was Maxine's turn, but she couldn't very well say that she'd taken the position to spend time with Heath Barton. So she went the bald-faced-lie route and explained that she'd wanted a job that involved singing, since she was into music. She also mumbled something about wanting to afford a certain dress, but that reason didn't seem quite as noble as making it home for Christmas.

❊   ❊   ❊

But at closing time on December 23, Maxine didn't care about being noble. Because that evening—the evening before their last official day—Sandy was handing out paychecks. As soon as Maxine received the flat envelope, she bid her coworkers good night and tore downstairs into the employee changing room. She had two clear goals, and they flashed before her like road signs: *Bank. Dress. Bank. Dress.* The boutique was still open for another thirty minutes. She was going to make this happen; she hadn't suffered for six days in vain.

The downstairs salespeople were quietly organizing stacks of handbags as Maxine thundered past them, her burnt-orange peacoat flapping behind her. She was zeroing in on the double doors when Heath Barton suddenly appeared and blocked her way.

"You can't leave now," Heath told her, holding up the palm of one hand and smiling devilishly. "I forbid you."

Maxine hadn't seen Heath yet that day and normally would have welcomed any excuse to return his playful banter. But tonight was an exception. She crossed her arms over her chest. "Heath, stop it. I have to be somewhere."

"Not in those ears you don't," Heath shot back, his grin deepening.

"Wha—?" Maxine touched the sides of her head to confirm, and sure enough, her pointy friends were still in place. Trying not to blush, Maxine yanked them off and crammed them into her messenger bag. She could well imagine the sight she would have made.

Citywide police alert! There's a fugitive elf running up Fifth Avenue!

"Listen, Maxine," Heath said, and he moved in close to her, so close that she could feel the warmth coming off him and smell his smoke-and-cider scent. Maxine's pulse had already been going nuts from her mad dash through Barton's; now it shot up to an emergency-room rate. "I talked to Mr. Perry today, so we're on for lunch tomorrow," Heath continued, his voice deep and private. "I'll come pick you up around noon?"

Finally! Maxine felt a swell of anticipation as she met Heath's gaze. What a glorious way to celebrate her last day at Barton's. She hoped they'd go someplace cozy and low-lit, maybe with a fireplace and waiters serving something gross-but-fancy, like caviar on toast. It would be, quite simply, the best lunch of Maxine Silver's life. "Sounds good," she told Heath, trying to keep her tone neutral.

Heath nodded, and a look of gratitude passed over his handsome face. "Terrific," he said. "There's something I've been wanting to ask you for a long time, and, well——" He smiled and pushed a hand through his black hair. "You'll see tomorrow."

Oh . . . my . . . God. Maybe it was because The Dress was mere heartbeats away, but suddenly Maxine knew what Heath wanted to ask her. "Is it about New Year's?" she whispered. It all made sense, didn't it? Heath hadn't brought up Tara's party before, so he was clearly waiting for the two of them to be alone . . . so he could ask Maxine to be his date. Maxine felt dizzy with luck and surprise. Everything she had worked toward this week was coming together in one moment of pure joy.

Heath's mouth lifted in a half smile. "I guess, in part," he replied mysteriously. "Hey, look," he added before Maxine could press him further, and he glanced up at the doorframe under which they stood. "Mistletoe."

Maxine followed his gaze and, sure enough, there it was, a slender green sprig tied with a red bow, hanging innocently over the Barton's entrance. On all her trips in and out of the store, Maxine had never noticed it, but then again, the boy she was dying to kiss had never been standing directly underneath it. "Oh," Maxine managed, feeling her cheeks color. Suddenly, making it to The Dress in time was the last thing on her mind.

"We must obey the mistletoe, right?" Heath asked teasingly. Putting one hand on Maxine's waist, he drew her close, angled his face down toward hers, and kissed her on the lips. His mouth tasted like apples and coffee. Then Heath pulled back, grinning at her. "Sorry—you were rushing off somewhere?" he asked, and then stepped out of the way.

Face burning, heart thudding, Maxine staggered outside. The sharp night wind, carrying the scent of roasted chestnuts, whipped at her, pedestrians pushed past her, and a street musician made his saxophone wail, but Maxine noticed none of it. All she could feel was the tingling of her own lips and the heat of her skin. God, it was almost torturous to have gotten such a small taste of Heath's kisses. Maybe at lunch tomorrow, after telling her how he felt about her and asking her to Tara's party, he'd lean over the caviar on toast and kiss her again. And then there'd be New Year's Eve: champagne corks popping, white and gold balloons, Heath in a suit, his hand on her lower back, his lips against hers . . .

Now all she needed was the outfit that would make that night complete.

Maxine floated over to the nearest bank branch, deposited her check in the ATM, and then flew up Columbus Avenue to the boutique, where the dress waited, glowing, in the window. Maxine grabbed eagerly for the door handle, but a frosty blonde young woman—*my sister in sales*, Maxine thought with a flash of sympathy—began locking the door from the inside, firmly shaking her head.

"Oh, come *on!*" Maxine cried, hopping up and down. "Two seconds!" Once one had sung Christmas carols while wearing elf tights, she realized, shame wasn't really such an issue in life anymore.

Rolling her eyes, the salesgirl cracked open the door for Maxine, who rushed in and made straight for the corner rack, where—*whew*—her size was still available. She paid for the dress with her debit card, relishing the knowledge that she now had more than enough in her account to cover it. Hell, she finally had enough to buy holiday gifts for everyone. Tomorrow, she'd put her Barton's discount to good use and get perfume for her mom, cuff links for Scott, and something extra-special-fancy for Tara.

❄   ❄   ❄

"Okay, start over!" Tara exclaimed on the phone that night. Maxine had called her, giddy and babbling, as soon as she'd left the boutique, but Tara had been hanging holly and had had to call back. Now, she'd caught Maxine just as she was modeling The Dress in front of her mirror.

"What do you want to hear about first—Heath or The Dress?" Maxine teased, peeking at herself over one shoulder. Her clothes from the day were strewn across her bed, and her Spotify playlist was on at full volume, drowning out her mom's and Scott's cello playing in the living room. They were rehearsing for their upcoming concert *again*.

"Duh." Tara laughed. "So he kissed you, and then he said—"

"No, *first* he said he had something to ask me, possibly related to New Year's, and then . . ." Maxine trailed off, beaming.

"Max." Tara's voice was quivery with excitement. "You know what this means, don't you? Heath *likes* you. This is *huge*. You're going to date Heath Barton!"

"I'm going to date Heath Barton," Maxine repeated softly, smiling at herself in the mirror as a thrill raced through her. "Tar, I know—can you *believe* it?"

"Well, I'll get to *see* it at my party." Tara laughed, and Maxine pictured her friend sitting on her grandparents' window seat, her chin on her knees as she watched the snow fall. Though it had been blizzarding in Oregon, it hadn't snowed in New York even once this winter. "And now you have The Dress," Tara went on. "So is your life complete?"

Is it? Maxine felt a sudden tug in the pit of her stomach. Her smile faded slightly as she studied her reflection. Was she the kind of girl who needed a dress, or shoes, or any store-bought treat to know true bliss? Since when had her winter break—her *life*—boiled down to the pursuit of material things? Maxine thought of the customers at Barton's, all hunting for what they hoped would make their Christmas complete, and an unexpected sadness washed over her. Maybe Heath had been right; everything was about bills, bills, bills in the end. But Maxine was no longer sure if she wanted to be a part of all that.

Then Maxine glanced down at her dress, admiring how its pale gold sheen caught the light, and she shrugged off her moment of brooding. She'd have plenty of time for deep thoughts *after* Heath saw her in The Dress on New Year's Eve. For now, she could simply revel in the glory.

"Max? You there?" Tara was asking. "Did Heath just sweep into your room and, like, propose to you?"

"Ask me that tomorrow." Maxine laughed, flopping back on her bed. "But wait—you won't be able to talk tomorrow night, right? It'll be Christmas Eve."

"Yup," Tara said. "For the next forty-eight hours, I'll be knee-deep in family duties like pretending to eat my grandmother's turkey, keeping my cousins from opening their gifts early, making sure my uncle doesn't drink too much eggnog . . ."

"Sounds better than my non-Christmas." Maxine sighed. "Mom and Scott are having some of their Philharmonic friends over tomorrow night to play chamber music. Then on Christmas Day, *no one* is going to be around."

Tara chuckled. "Oh, please. You'll be so happy after your lunch with Heath that you won't *want* to do anything but lie on your bed and stare dreamily into space—which I'm sure is what you're doing right now."

"Merry Christmas, Tar," Maxine said, and blew a kiss into the phone.

Grinning, she stretched across the bed in her gold dress. It was almost midnight, and excitement shot through her. She was in no rush for it to be Christmas, but tomorrow couldn't come fast enough.

❄   ❄   ❄

After managing a few hours of sleep, Maxine headed to Barton's with more energy than she'd ever had on an early work morning. But she needed every ounce of it, because that day, everyone in New York City seemed to be on a mission to buy out the Christmas Corner before nightfall. In between managing the madness and slinking away to buy her holiday gifts, Maxine was caught off guard by noon's arrival. She had just enough time to change out of her elf gear and into her denim skirt, a mocha-colored sweater, and platform boots.

"Wow, you look great," Heath said when they met by the chocolate snowmen. Holding his ubiquitous Starbucks cup in one hand, he put the other on Maxine's arm and gave her a kiss on the cheek, stirring up delicious memories from last night. Maxine wished Sandy had hung some mistletoe in the Corner—it seemed to be the *only* Christmas decoration not present.

"But you didn't need to change," Heath added, pulling back. "We're only going upstairs."

"We are?" Maxine asked, disappointment pricking her like a needle. *Upstairs* was the third floor, which Sandy referred to as the "Cruise Wear" department—the section for those lucky few who traveled to warm climes in the winter. Curious, Maxine followed Heath up the winding staircase to the third level—and felt like she had landed on another planet. Maxine gazed around in wonder at sherbet-colored bikinis, sparkly flip-flops, and flowery sarongs. Unlike the level below them, this floor was hushed and empty, with nary a customer or salesperson in sight. Maxine's breath quickened. Had Heath brought her up here so they could be utterly alone? Maybe any second he'd turn to her, wrap an arm around her waist, and whisper that ever since high school, he'd been kind of in love with—

"Ever since high school," Heath spoke, and Maxine gave a start, "I've noticed that you have a great sense of style." Before a blushing Maxine could modestly wave him off, Heath gestured to a stack of bikinis on a table and added, "So I figured you'd be the best girl to give me advice on these."

Maxine frowned, confusion muddying her glee.

Heath lifted up a pink-and-black bikini, studying it closely. "This would look really hot on Julianne because she's all tan and whatnot, but do you think it's too trendy?" He shot a worried glance at Maxine. "Julianne already has a lot of designer stuff, so I wanted to get her something more unique for Christmas, you know?"

Maxine felt a coldness seep into her limbs. *Who's Julianne?* she almost whispered, but she already knew. She knew, with a certainty that made her chest seize up, that Heath Barton had asked her here to help him pick out a bikini for his girlfriend. So *that* was what he'd been wanting to ask her for a long time. Maxine had thought she'd done away with shame but now she felt it flooding her face, consuming her completely.

"Why—um—why a bikini?" Maxine asked, hoping her voice didn't sound as shaky to Heath as it did to her ears. She felt she had to ask *something* in order to beat down the other questions rising inside her. As in: *Why did you act like you were into me, you jerk?*

"Oh, I didn't tell you?" Heath asked, now rifling through the bikinis and picking out a lemon-yellow one. "My parents and I always fly down to our place in Anguilla on Christmas Eve, and this year Julianne's meeting us there. She's flying in from Aspen, so I'm sure she won't have bought a new bikini there." He looked up at Maxine. "Do you like the yellow more?"

"You spend Christmas in Anguilla?" Maxine felt that as long as she kept talking, she'd manage to avoid bursting into tears of humiliation. Had she really believed—all this time—

"Family tradition," Heath replied as he examined a zebra-print two-piece. "We stay through New Year's too, so"—he gave her a sheepish smile—"that was the other thing I wanted to ask you. I know your friend's having a party, and obviously I won't be able to make it. Can you let her know? I got her invite but I think I deleted it by accident."

A great wave of hurt crested over Maxine. She thought of The Dress, waiting in her closet, and feared that sobbing might be around the corner. "But—but Anguilla isn't all that Christmasy," she managed in a choked voice, when what she really wanted to say was *Thanks for ruining my winter break*. "I thought you guys would go to, like, London since your dad's British and all." She swallowed hard, willing her eyes not to tear.

Heath snorted, momentarily forgetting the bikinis. "British? He was born in Staten Island. His real name's Charlie Barstein— oh, but don't tell anyone, 'kay?" He turned to Maxine and held up the zebra bikini. "Too much?" he asked.

Maxine shook her head, speechless. What was *too much* was her realization that everything about Barton's—from its name to its owner to its hot young heir—was fake. Maxine took a step back, looking Heath up and down as if she were noticing him for the first time. In truth, the suave, sexy Heath Barton was nothing more than a spoiled rich boy with only one true love: himself. He hadn't had a thing for her, Maxine understood. She'd been just another quick flirtation—another girl who would inflate his ego while his girlfriend was away. That was all. What a fool Maxine had been. A silly, lovestruck, elf fool.

"You *kissed* me," Maxine spoke up, finding her voice and her courage at the same time. Steadier now, she met Heath's bewildered gaze. "You kissed me, but you have a girlfriend. How is that cool?"

Heath blinked at her. "Uh, hello, Maxine—mistletoe?" He said this as if she were overlooking the world's most obvious fact.

Mistletoe. Now it was anger that rushed through Maxine, quelling the threat of tears. She was sick of mistletoe and tinsel and all the trappings of the season. She was *done* with Barton's, and with the Christmas Corner. But she'd never have even been here in the first place if it weren't for Heath. At this realization, Maxine felt a fresh surge of fury.

"You know what?" she began, glaring at Heath. "It doesn't matter what bikini you get Julianne, does it? Because within a year she'll probably figure out how self-absorbed and arrogant you are, or you'll cheat on her or something, and she'll wind up returning all your meaningless gifts anyway." She took a deep breath, backing up toward the staircase as Heath watched her, slack-jawed. "So now, if you'll excuse me, I, unlike you, have a *job* to do."

Fuming, Maxine whirled around and started down the staircase. Heath remained silent and immobile behind her, but just as she reached the second level, she heard him call out to her.

"Hang on," Heath said, leaning over the banister with the bikinis still in hand. Maxine was pleased to see that he looked ruffled and out of sorts, and hoped some of what she'd said had sunk in. Then Heath spoke again. "You never told me which one you liked better."

Maxine stared up at him in disbelief. "The zebra," she finally replied. "It's kind of expensive-tacky—like you." With that, she stormed into the Christmas Corner, promptly bumping into Avery, who was carrying a stack of Santa suits to the cash register.

"Whoa, is everything all right?" Avery asked, raising his eyebrows at her.

Ugh. The last thing she needed now was Avery's sympathy—which was probably all an act anyway. "Oh, like you care," Maxine snapped, brushing past him without a second thought.

For the first time in her Barton's career, Maxine was grateful to change into her elf costume. She was shaking with anger, replaying the ugly scene with Heath in her head. So it was a relief to throw herself back into work, even if that work involved tearing apart two grown women who were wrestling over a chocolate snowman, and then fumbling through a performance of "The Little Drummer Boy."

The Corner grew more crowded as the afternoon progressed. It didn't help that Claudette danced off early to catch her plane to Houston, hugging everyone and promising to stay in touch but clearly thrilled to be getting out of there. By the time seven o'clock—the normal closing hour—rolled around, Maxine was starving (she'd never eaten), sweaty, and ready to settle down for a long winter's nap. When Sandy rounded up her, Daniel, and Avery for an impromptu meeting, Maxine hoped that it was to tell them they were free to leave, despite the fact that the place was still a mob scene.

But Sandy delivered the opposite news. "The word's come down from Mr. Perry: We're staying open until nine," she announced grimly, peering at her employees over her clipboard. "I expect each of you to remain here and help close up."

"Dude, no can do—I'm catching a nine-o'clock flight at JFK," Daniel spoke up, looking more alert than Maxine had ever seen him. "I assumed we'd get off early on our last day, and—"

Before Sandy could bark at Daniel, Avery spoke up. "I can stay, but just until eight," he offered, removing his boxy Nutcracker hat and running a hand through his blond hair. "There's something I need to—"

"I get it, I get it," Sandy snapped, putting one hand on her hip. "What can I expect on Christmas Eve?" She shot a glance at Maxine. "And you, Elf?"

Maxine opened her mouth, ready to invent some fib about catching a plane, train, or automobile—but then realized she didn't want to. The truth was, she had no place to be on Christmas Eve and, in a twisted way, closing up the Corner would be preferable to enduring a lame night at home: live chamber music emanating from the living room, her mom and Scott snuggling, Maxine locked in her bedroom, seething over Heath Barton . . .

"I'll stay," Maxine said, squaring her shoulders.

"Well, it's the least you can do considering you took a long lunch today," Sandy replied, by way of thanking her.

"Maxine, righteous of you to stay the course," Daniel said, giving her a good-bye kiss on the cheek and knocking fists with Avery. "We'll be forever grateful."

Maxine shrugged. "I'm a Hanukkah kind of girl anyway, so it's not like I've got big Christmas plans," she said. Then she waved to Daniel and headed for the gift wrap counter, where Sandy was beckoning to her and Avery.

For the next hour, as Maxine worked the Christmas Corner alongside Avery, she felt some of her fury ebbing away. She and Avery actually made a solid team, he handing her a tube of wrapping paper just when she was reaching for it, she passing him the scissors before he could ask for them. It was Avery who kept the customers calm while Maxine hunted for hard-to-find items; once, after managing to quiet a bellowing grandpa with the right snow globe, the two of them exchanged a relieved grin, and Maxine felt a pang of regret over how she'd dismissed him earlier. Avery may have been studying acting in school, but, as Maxine observed him across the store—patiently listening to a panicked dad, saluting on command for a group of giggling girls—she realized that the sparkle in his blue-gray eyes and the warmth in his smile were entirely genuine.

Maxine was kneeling beneath the gift wrap counter, retrieving a Barton's box and wondering if she should apologize to him, when Avery leaned over the counter.

"It's, um, almost eight," he said awkwardly, turning his boxy Nutcracker hat around and around in his hands. "I should— you know—"

"It's okay," Maxine said, getting to her feet. "Have a merry—"

"So, um, I guess I'll see you," Avery said abruptly, lifting one hand in farewell and backing off in a hurry.

He hates me, Maxine decided, watching him go. She wished she'd at least told him that he was maybe the only guy who could pull off looking that good in a Nutcracker costume. But now, considering he was headed home to Illinois for Christmas, she'd probably never see him again. Melancholy settled over Maxine like a dusting of snow, and she focused again on the line of impatient customers.

At five to nine, Sandy finally granted Maxine her freedom and, looking as though she were in pain, thanked her for a job well done. Instead of feeling footloose and festive, though, Maxine found herself fighting down a lump in her throat. Slowly, she changed out of her elf clothes for the very last time, slipped on her coat, hat, and scarf, and scooped up her messenger bag full of holiday gifts. She made her way through the silent ground level, and the security guard locked the door behind her as she stepped outside.

Good-bye, Barton's.

Maxine stood by herself on Fifth Avenue, breathing in the wintry air. As she drew her coat collar up, she lifted her eyes to the giant twinkling snowflake, which, in the nighttime gloom, suddenly seemed very lonely. *Or maybe that's just me*, Maxine thought, swallowing hard. Rather than heading for home, she turned and began meandering down the empty avenue, past the tall designer shops. The stores' holiday windows—white lights twined around silvery branches, elaborately designed dolls arranged in scenes from *A Christmas Carol*—were incongruously bright against the darkness. Maxine thought she heard laughter and the sound of glasses clinking coming from a window high above, but she couldn't place the source of the merriment. A lone taxicab shot past, startling her; its windows were rolled down, and the song "All Alone on Christmas" blasted out into the night.

"The cold wind is blowin' and the streets are getting dark . . . nobody ought to be all alone on Christmas."

The song capped everything off; Maxine stopped in the middle of Fifth Avenue, buried her face in her mittened hands, and surrendered to the tears that had been building ever since she'd learned the truth about Heath that afternoon. As the warm, salty drops fell, Maxine, who didn't cry all that often, let herself wallow in self-pity. She'd had an awful day, but this moment was worse than anything that had happened back at Barton's—because she felt like the only person alive not celebrating somewhere. The shops, the decorations, and the music were not for her. Standing in the heart of her hometown—in a city packed with so many interesting and quirky people who celebrated all varieties of holidays—Maxine Silver had somehow never felt so adrift.

"I don't think Sandy would approve."

A voice at her side made Maxine glance up and instinctively tug her bag against her. But the person standing beside her was not a Christmas Eve mugger. It was Avery Prince.

"I mean, that's not much holiday cheer you're showing, is it?" Avery clarified, and though his tone was playful, concern darkened his blue-gray eyes.

"Oh, um, I guess not." Maxine sniffled, rubbing the tears off her cheeks. She wished he hadn't seen her crying. But what was he even *doing* here? Maxine blinked, noticing that Avery was holding two cups topped with whipped cream and wearing a bomber jacket over a navy-blue sweater and corduroys. It was the first time Maxine had ever seen Avery out of his Nutcracker gear and, in spite of herself, her heart skipped a beat. There had been something adorable about Avery in costume, but seeing him now, the word that came to mind was *beautiful*. His high cheekbones, cornsilk hair, the dimple in his left cheek when he smiled . . . how had Maxine never picked up on it before?

"I'm sorry if I startled you—I stopped by Barton's first," Avery was explaining. "But then I saw you standing down here, so . . ." He lifted one shoulder, his smile shy.

Maxine's head spun as she tried to piece together what Avery was saying. "You . . . you were looking for *me*?" she stammered. "But why—I thought you were going home—"

Avery shook his head, extending one of the cups toward Maxine. "I didn't have time to make travel arrangements this year. Flights to Chicago book up so fast." He paused, and his eyes swept over Maxine's face, making her breath catch a little. "Here," he added softly. "You seem like you could use some hot cocoa."

"No kidding," Maxine said gratefully, accepting the cup from Avery. She was reminded of the morning he had brought in mochas for the group; he really *was* a thoughtful guy. Maxine blew on the steaming surface, then took a sip. The rich, sweet liquid warmed her to the core and seemed to sate her hunger. Avery, too, was sipping his drink, and as he and Maxine looked at each other over their respective brims, Maxine could feel herself start to smile.

Without a word, the two of them turned and slowly began walking south on Fifth, their elbows touching each time they lifted their cups to their lips. Whenever this happened, Maxine felt a tingle move up her arm, and she wondered if Avery was feeling the same thing. As they walked on, with the lights from the store windows illuminating their path, they began to talk, their breath forming clouds on the air. They laughed over Sandy's clipboard, dissected Daniel's spaciness, and debated whether or not Claudette could ever be clumsy. Somehow discussing Barton's with Avery made Maxine feel worlds better, and she was surprised to learn that even he had some issues with the job.

"So how did you do it?" Maxine asked him as they approached Rockefeller Center. "You always seemed so . . . glad to be there."

Avery glanced at her with a half smile. "Trust me, Maxine, I had my down moments, just like you. But I try to make the best of things. I know, I know." He laughed as Maxine wrinkled her nose. "Cue the corniness, right? But I never really *minded* Barton's.

After all, if I didn't work there, I wouldn't have met—" Avery paused and drank from his cocoa again, his face reddening.

Me? Maxine thought, her stomach giving a jump. She was still feeling too unsteady to pose such a bold question, so instead she simply nodded, clutching her cocoa cup.

"But the commercialism of this time of year does get to me," Avery added thoughtfully, as he and Maxine turned into Rockefeller Center. The colorful flags flapped in the wind, the tree glowed, and the golden statue of Prometheus watched over the pure-white rink. Only a smattering of ice skaters were zipping around tonight. "Everyone's so hung up on buying stuff . . ." As they reached the ledge that overlooked the rink, Avery gazed down at the skaters, the light from below casting shadows on his profile.

Maxine glanced at Avery, surprised that he had echoed her thoughts from the night before. Maybe they had more in common than Maxine had first thought. "So what's the alternative?" Maxine teased, playing devil's advocate. She gave Avery a nudge, thinking how much more relaxed she was around him, as opposed to, say, Heath Barton. "A holiday without gifts? Horrors!"

Avery turned to her, smiling and shaking his head. "Well, gifts can also be, like . . . moments instead of things, you know?" he asked, then bit his lip. "Does that make sense?"

Like this moment, Maxine caught herself thinking, and a warmth that had nothing to do with the hot cocoa spread through her body. Suddenly she felt something wet land on her cheek, and then her nose, and Maxine tilted her head up, laughing. Glistening white flakes were swirling down from the sky—the first snowfall of the year. From the skating rink below, Maxine heard people break out into cheers of appreciation.

Avery, too, looked up and laughed, and then glanced back at Maxine. "Is New York City always this postcard-perfect in the winter?" he asked, setting down his cocoa cup and attempting to catch the dancing flakes in his hands.

"We try," Maxine replied, blinking snowflakes off her lashes, and realizing that Avery's wide-eyed enthusiasm wasn't getting on her nerves this time. It was actually kind of fun to experience the city with a non-native. "Wait," Maxine added, remembering something Avery had said earlier. "If you weren't going back to Illinois tonight, why did you have to leave early?"

"Oh." Avery looked down abruptly, his cheeks flushing again, and Maxine felt a sudden wave of nervousness that warmed her own face. "I, um, well, now that you ask . . . I was going to get you something," he said.

"You were?" Maxine asked breathlessly, and then pointed to her empty cocoa cup on the ledge. "You mean . . . this?"

Avery shook his head, still studying the snow-dusted ground. "Nah—I got those after the original plan didn't work out." Slowly, Avery raised his eyes until he met Maxine's gaze. "I went to Lincoln Center to get us . . . tickets. Tickets to the New York Philharmonic's concert next week." He let out a big breath, looking crestfallen. "But it was sold out."

Maxine clapped a hand over her mouth, unable to stop her burst of laughter. What were the chances? "Avery, you didn't need to do that!" she exclaimed, feeling as dizzy and carefree as the snowflakes tumbling around her. When he shook his head politely, Maxine clarified. "No, I mean, you *really* didn't have to do that. I know it's random, but my mom and stepdad are *in* the Philharmonic. They're going to play in that concert, and they can totally get us tickets." Normally Maxine wouldn't have been excited by the prospect of one of her mom's concerts, but the thought of going with Avery, of seeing him again outside Barton's, made her pulse flutter.

"That is exceptionally cool," Avery declared, his face lighting up with relief. "You must get to hear amazing music all the time."

"Eh," Maxine replied, making a so-so motion with her hand. "Classical's not my favorite." When Avery nodded in agreement, Maxine added, "So what made you think of the Philharmonic, then?"

Avery grinned, lifting one shoulder. "Well, you mentioned once you loved music. So I figured you'd enjoy something more, I don't know, peaceful after all that Christmas carol *mishegas* we had to go through." He rolled his eyes for emphasis.

"Um . . . what did you just say?" Maxine asked, wondering if the snowfall had affected her hearing.

"*Mishegas?*" Avery repeated, grinning. "You know, it's Yiddish. It means craziness or whatever——"

"I know," Maxine cut him off, now thoroughly confused. "It's my Grandma Rose's favorite expression but——"

"My grandma's too," Avery said matter-of-factly, brushing his blond hair back off his forehead.

"But Avery—" Maxine sputtered as the implications of his words hit home. "I thought—don't you celebrate Christmas?"

Avery shook his head, his eyes sparkling. "I *like* Christmas a lot, but I guess you'd say I'm a Hanukkah kind of guy." He stuck his hands in his pockets. "Happy Hanukkah, by the way—even though it's been over for a couple of days now."

Maxine's lips parted in amazement. Avery Prince was . . . *Jewish*? She thought about how isolated she'd felt in all that Christmas madness, when all along, of all people . . . And suddenly, it made perfect sense that Avery had met her on lonesome Fifth Avenue, and now stood with her in a quiet, sparkling Rockefeller Center. He didn't have Christmas Eve plans, either. She wasn't so alone after all.

"What are you thinking, Maxine Silver?" Avery asked, flashing her an intrigued smile and taking a step closer to her.

"Oh . . . nothing." Maxine laughed, looking up at him. "Just that I'm never going to assume something about anyone ever again."

Avery nodded, holding her gaze, and then his expression turned serious—intense. Through the steady snowfall, Maxine watched him study her, and her heart tapped against her ribs. "What are *you* thinking?" she volleyed back at him.

"Just that . . ." Avery reached over and brushed a snowflake off the tip of Maxine's nose. "When you're not dressed like an elf, you're even more beautiful."

Maxine felt her face grow hotter than it ever had under Heath Barton's gaze. Heath's compliments had been flip and fleeting, but she could sense the earnestness behind Avery's words. And for once, Maxine was speechless. All she could do was step forward and meet Avery as he was stepping closer to her. No mistletoe was necessary; the moment alone told them what to do. Maxine let her eyes drift shut as Avery lowered his face and kissed her, soft and slow. *I'm kissing the Nutcracker Prince*, Maxine thought as she felt Avery's warm lips claim hers, but instead of laughing, she kissed him back, savoring every second. The way their mouths fit together, the way Avery's arms went around her waist right as hers went around his neck, seemed to cancel out any kiss—or any moment—she'd shared with Heath Barton.

"You idiot." Maxine sighed when they broke apart, resting her fingers against Avery's lips. "Why didn't you do that *days* ago?"

Avery laughed, shaking his head. "Maxine, I thought you had written me off from the start. When I met you, you were so, I don't know, sharp and funny, and that was what I liked about you, but it also made me nervous . . ." He glanced down, clearly embarrassed. "And then you were always talking with Heath Barton, so I figured . . ."

"You figured wrong," Maxine whispered, standing on her toes to kiss Avery's cheek. Heath seemed very far away now, and not only because he was off in Anguilla. Maxine's crush on him felt distant, faded around the edges, like an old photograph.

Holding hands, Avery and Maxine turned and left Rockefeller Center and, as the snow continued to drift down, wound their way toward Maxine's apartment building. When they reached the green awning on 79th Street, they lingered on the corner, far from the curious gaze of Maxine's doorman. Avery had to head back downtown to his NYU dorm but first there were matters to discuss.

"If you're around tomorrow," Avery murmured, lacing his fingers through Maxine's, his warm breath tickling her ear. "Would you be up for a movie and Chinese food?"

"Of course." Maxine laughed. "The Jewish tradition. What else is there to do on Christmas, right?"

"Well . . . this, for one," Avery whispered. Gently, he lifted Maxine's chin and started kissing her once more. Then Maxine's hands were in Avery's hair, and he was clutching the back of her coat to draw her in closer. Avery—who knew? Maxine would have never guessed that someone so polite could kiss so well.

"So speaking of plans," Maxine murmured against Avery's lips, smiling. "If *you're* around on New Year's Eve, I know of a certain fabulous party . . ." Her heart soared as she thought of The Dress; now *here* was a boy worthy of seeing her in it.

"I'm there," Avery replied, playfully tugging Maxine's hat down over her eyes.

As she and Avery started kissing again, under the falling snow and the light from a lamppost, Maxine suddenly felt like the whole city—from the shimmery decorations to the Christmas carols drifting down from an apartment window—was all for her tonight. All for *them*. And that realization, combined with the feel of Avery's arms around her, was as sweet and warm and satisfying as a holiday song.

THE MAGI'S GIFTS

BY MELISSA DE LA CRUZ

"**T**here he is," Kelsey Cooper said, spotting her boyfriend's shaggy dark head above the crowd of people exiting the annual *Joy to the World: Parker High Christmas Concert Extravaganza*. "Over here!" she called, waving her program in the air. Her breath caught in her throat the same way it did every time she saw him.

Tall, broad-shouldered, and still tan from working outdoors at his grandparents' apple orchard during the autumn harvest, Brenden Molloy had cheekbones to rival a Hollywood star's and blue-green eyes that sparkled with wicked fun. He would be the cutest guy in school if it weren't for tousled bangs that obscured half of his face. His hair was so long it curled underneath his ears and licked his shirt collar.

He shot her a quick grin as he walked over to Kelsey and her friend Gigi McClusky, taking graceful, loping strides, cradling his saxophone in its black case.

Instead of saying hello, Kelsey rushed up and pushed his hair back from his forehead.

"Hi to you, too," he teased.

Kelsey sighed. Brenden had looked so nice earlier in his concert uniform——a black tuxedo——and part of her secretly wished that he could look like that all the time: not necessarily in black tie, but just a bit more polished and cleaned up than usual. He had already changed into his usual attire of holey concert T-shirt, battered jean jacket, weathered cotton Dickies, and thick-soled black combat boots. With his messy hair and collection of thick black armbands, he looked seriously grungy. Hot, but grungy.

In contrast, Kelsey was meticulously put together, as if she'd stepped off the pages of a glossy magazine, from her seashell-pink manicure to her tailored fur-trimmed red car coat. She was slim, with fair, clear, cornflower-blue eyes, burnished, honey-brown hair with strawberry-blonde highlights, and skin that tanned easily during the summer, sprinkling freckles across her nose and cheeks. Like Brenden, she was sixteen years old, and a junior at Parker.

"You were awesome!" Kelsey beamed. Brenden was first-chair saxophone——a big deal, since six kids who played the same instrument had vied for the same spot.

"Bravo!" their English teacher, Mrs. Townsend, interjected as she passed by, smiling warmly at Brenden. The Christmas recital was a town favorite——even the mayor never missed a performance.

"Yeah, cool *solo*," Gigi drawled, although from her tone of voice it was obvious that she thought playing the interlude to "White Christmas" for the school orchestra was far from "cool."

"Thanks," Brenden mumbled, looking down at his boots.

Kelsey glanced from her boyfriend to her friend with a rising feeling of panic, wishing that they would miraculously find some way to get along. She should have known it had been a mistake to invite Gigi to the concert.

Gigi McClusky was the head of the Wade Hill crowd, a group of rich, snobby kids who all lived in the same ritzy part of town and had all attended the same small, private elementary school within the gated community. They were traditionally sent to boarding schools back east to prep for college, but recently a large, and growing, contingent were sent to Parker High. Until they'd arrived, Kelsey had never known there was anything wrong with her Target wardrobe, her dad's ten-year-old Chrysler, or her trusty backpack. But the Wade Hill kids were dropped off in their parents' BMW SUVs, shopped at Saks Fifth Avenue in the mall, and toted bags made of calfskin instead of canvas.

They had welcomed Kelsey into their ranks even though Kelsey wasn't rich, snobby, or from Wade Hill. (Her fur-trimmed coat was a knockoff.) But she was prettier than the whole lot of them put together, and after all, they couldn't call themselves the Beautiful People if they didn't count the most beautiful girl in school among them.

Kelsey laced her arm through Brenden's and gave it a squeeze. She would rather have kissed him but knew he was slightly embarrassed by PDA. He rarely even held her hand when they were out together. She wished he would be more demonstrative in public, although he more than made up for it when they were alone.

"Seriously, Bren, you guys rocked," she said, a little too enthusiastically, hoping to smooth over Gigi's passive-aggressive burn.

"Yep, we turned it all the way up to eleven," Brenden deadpanned, making a reference to their favorite movie, *This Is Spinal Tap*. The image of the Parker High orchestra populated by aging British metalheads made Kelsey giggle, and soon she and Brenden were laughing at the shared joke while Gigi stood uncomfortably to the side.

"Well, I should go!" Gigi announced abruptly. "I told my dad I'd be home early tonight. There's so much work we still need to do for the party!" She tossed her long, shiny, ebony-black hair over her shoulder. "Bye-yee," she said, leaning over and affectedly kissing the air two inches away from each of Kelsey's cheeks while Kelsey did the same to her. "Mwah! Mwah!"

Brenden tried not to roll his eyes. "Tell me again how you can stand her?" he grumbled, as they walked out of the auditorium through the revolving glass doors to the parking lot.

"She's my *friend*," Kelsey said tightly. "She's *nice* to me."

He shrugged, dropping the subject for once, and Kelsey was relieved. Brenden thought Gigi was a shallow airhead and typically didn't hold back from telling Kelsey so, but it was too beautiful an evening for quarreling. Outside, a pristine blanket of snow covered everything from the old slate shingles on the building rooftops to the surrounding meadows and towering fir trees. The air smelled fresh and brisk, scented by the earthy, rich fragrance of pine.

"I love it here." Kelsey sighed.

There was nothing special about Parker, Ohio—it was such a small town that its main drag consisted of a lone bank, beauty salon, and pizza parlor, as well as the three squat buildings that made up the entire public school system. An hour and a half away from Cleveland and forty-five minutes from the nearest mall, its most famous resident was a girl who'd tried out for a singing contest on TV last season but got cut on the first round. But every year during Christmas, Kelsey thought it was the best place in the world.

Across the street from the high school, the little wooden gazebo in the middle of the town square was decorated with evergreen garlands heavy with red holly berries and white mistletoe sprays. An enormous wreath festooned with silver pinecones hung over the entrance to the City Hall, and twinkling white lights wrapped around the candy-cane-colored barbershop poles added to the festive sight.

"It looks like a Hallmark card," Kelsey said. "In a good way."

"You say that every year." Brenden smiled.

"I know, but it's true."

Brenden nodded at the wisdom of that statement. "Hey, what's over there?" he asked, putting his saxophone case on the ground and motioning toward the distance. Kelsey swiveled to look to where he was pointing, only to feel a shock of something cold and wet on the back of her neck.

"Oh, no, you *didn't*!" she squealed, shaking the snowball off. She immediately scooped a handful of snow with her gloved hands and plastered him in the face with it. Brenden hopped away, but Kelsey had a good arm and had soon pelted him with a half-dozen snowballs.

"Truce! Truce!" Brenden yelled, laughing hysterically as a volley of snowballs struck his torso. "I know you love to win."

"Remember in third grade when I put that walkie-talkie in your closet?" Kelsey said. "You thought your GI Joes were talking to you!"

"Remember in fifth grade when I hid that frog in your lunch-box?" he taunted, packing a snowball and aiming for her pitching arm. "You screamed for a week!"

"Did not!" she howled, momentarily rendered off-balance by his offensive strike. She scrambled onto the snowbanks to collect more ammunition.

They reached the far side of the school parking lot, still throwing snowballs at each other. Once they were alone, Brenden grabbed Kelsey by the waist and they fell down into the snow, the two of them tumbling on the ground and laughing.

"There," he said, brushing the snow off her hair.

She laughed breathlessly as Brenden put his arms and legs on top of hers, and began to wave them up and down to make a snow angel.

"That tickles!" Kelsey said, feeling the cold start to seep through her coat and sweater. But for once she wasn't worried about how her hair or her clothes looked. Brenden was the only guy she'd ever known who could make her laugh so hard her belly ached. "It's cold out here!" she gasped as a light snow began to fall, and the glow from the streetlights turned each snowflake into a flickering beacon.

In answer, Brenden leaned over her so that their faces were so close to each other that she could feel his breath on her cheek. "Still cold?" he whispered, his eyelashes fluttering on her forehead, his fingers intertwining with hers.

"No . . ." She lifted her lips up to him for a kiss, and their mouths met, and she could taste snowflakes on his tongue.

"You love me, Kelseygirl?" he asked, looking deep into her eyes.

"I love you, Brenden James Molloy," she whispered, pulling him closer so he could hear.

"Good, because I love you, too." He grinned, getting up and lifting her to her feet.

The very first time they'd kissed was one afternoon last summer when they were shooting hoops in Brenden's backyard. After he'd made several over-the-shoulder shots to flatten her 16–4, he'd turned to her and said, ultracasually, as if he were perusing a menu and ordering a hamburger, "I really like you." She'd blushed and said she didn't know what he was talking about; of course they liked each other—they were friends. They'd spent their childhoods bickering and teasing each other. Brenden had seen her sick with the chicken pox when they were five, and a few years later she was the only one who knew Brenden had cried when his parents split. So she didn't know what he was getting at until he put the basketball down and looked at her straight in the eye.

"No, I mean, I *like you* like you," he'd explained. Then he'd kissed her while the sun set behind the ravine, and he smelled like gum and coffee and tasted like something infinitely more delicious—like chocolate and boy-sweat, salty and sweet. It was the first and best kiss of her life. They were like Jennifer Garner and Mark Ruffalo in *13 Going on 30*, except they hadn't needed any magic wishing dust or a New York City idyll complete with Michael Jackson "Thriller" dance moves to find each other.

Now Brenden tenderly brushed the snow off her back, and they walked over to where he'd parked his motorcycle. Kelsey watched patiently as he secured his saxophone case in the rear rack with two bungee cords before climbing on herself.

"It's looking good. Did you get it detailed?" she asked, admiring his ride.

"Uh-huh, did it myself this afternoon." He smiled, handing over her helmet.

Brenden's bike was a vintage 1965 Hog, the one thing his dad had left him. It was his pride and joy—he kept it well oiled and in prime condition, the chrome polished to a reflective shine. Many people in town had offered him good money to take it off his hands but he always refused. Kelsey knew he would never trade that bike for anything. It was part of him; it made him who he was. Without the bike, he was just some poor kid in ripped jeans riding the yellow school bus. But with the bike he was Marlon Brando in *The Wild One*, Dennis Hopper in *Easy Rider*, an artist, a rebel, a hero.

He swung over to the front seat and rubbed his hands together for warmth as he shivered under his thin, tattered denim jacket. Kelsey felt a pang as she wrapped her arms around his waist.

She knew how much Brenden wished he could afford a proper leather motorcycle jacket, like the matte black one with the silver zippers they'd spied in the Harley-Davidson store in downtown Cleveland one afternoon. But the jacket cost more than four hundred dollars brand-new, and there was no way Brenden would ever have that kind of money. He worked part-time at a garage but all his paychecks went straight to the Stop & Shop to help his mom put food on the table. His father's alimony and child support checks never arrived on time, if at all.

But none of that mattered as Brenden kicked the Harley into gear and it revved up with a satisfying roar. As they drove off in the dusting snowfall, Kelsey pressed tightly against the strong back of the boy she loved, glad she was there to keep him warm.

School was out for winter break, so Kelsey dragged Brenden to the Parker Mall the next day, ostensibly because she had a coupon for Bed Bath & Beyond that she wanted to use to buy her mom a little something. Christmas was just a handful of days away. Sadly, with her meager allowance and the pittance she made babysitting, "a little something" was all she could afford for everyone on her Christmas list that year. But Kelsey was really at the mall to shop for *him*—she had saved up the most for Brenden's gift. Although she had no idea how she would be able to buy him a present that would show how much she loved him with only forty-five dollars—all she'd managed to scrape together and save.

Forty-five dollars! What could anyone buy for someone you loved with all your heart for only forty-five dollars? Kelsey wanted to buy him something truly wonderful, something that would show him how much he meant to her.

They walked past the roped-off Santa's House section, where crying kids were being escorted to sit on the bearded guy's lap. The mall was bursting with eager, last-minute shoppers who swarmed the stores, ignoring the Salvation Army bell-ringers and their red buckets. After a quick kiss good-bye, Brenden and Kelsey went their separate ways with the tacit knowledge that each was shopping for the other.

Kelsey walked desperately from store to store, feeling more and more discouraged at the dismal offerings her budget would allow. At the Sharper Image, she contemplated a battery-powered razor; at the Apple store, a pair of fancy earbuds; and at Banana Republic, wool sweaters were marked down to thirty bucks. But nothing seemed right. Too cheap, too generic, too lame—and certainly not worthy of someone as special as Brenden.

The lack of money in her pocket made Kelsey feel pensive, and not quite in the Christmas spirit. After a fruitless hour, she met up with Brenden at their designated meeting place in front of the Starbucks and found he was similarly empty-handed.

"Get anything?" he asked.

She shook her head grimly. Her mood didn't brighten when they walked by the food court and she noticed a bunch of Wade Hill girls—minus Gigi—holding court at a primo table. Brenden immediately began to study the fast-food menu overhead with focused concentration.

"Hey," Kelsey greeted them, trying not to feel self-conscious in front of Gigi's circle. She couldn't help but wonder if they ever noticed that her jeans didn't have the telltale wavy line stitched on the back pockets like theirs did.

"Hiiii, Kelsey," they cooed. "Hey, Brenden." The group of popular girls all looked alike, from their shiny straightened hair and whitened teeth, to their cozy cashmere sweaters, and their matching football-playing, clean-cut boyfriends in their varsity letter jackets and faded button-downs.

"Where's Gigi?" Kelsey asked, glancing around.

"I think she's out with her mom, getting her dress fitted," a girl named Sarah answered excitedly. "Did you know? She's getting her hair and makeup done for the party by some guy from Chicago! He has a salon in Paris, too! Her parents are flying him in! She's so lucky!" Sarah sighed, her eyes wide with envy.

Gigi's upcoming Christmas Eve Party/Sweet Sixteen Bash at the sprawling McClusky mansion was all anyone ever wanted to talk about ever since the invitations—embossed on creamy card stock as thick as cardboard—had landed in their mailboxes. The party was to be the biggest event the town had ever seen. The McCluskys had even hired a catering company and booked a DJ from Cleveland. To Kelsey, it sounded nothing short of magical, like one of those parties where the celebrant arrived at the event in a Cinderella carriage or hidden among a group of undulating belly dancers like she'd seen on MTV.

"Ehmagad, it'll be so pimped out!" another girl enthused. "She told me they're tenting the backyard!"

"They've invited everyone in town," said a third.

"Well, everyone who matters!" a fourth corrected.

They all looked at Kelsey with anticipation. "You *are* coming, right?"

"I—I guess so, I mean, of course," she replied, looking at Brenden meaningfully. But her boyfriend was acting as if memorizing all the ingredients of a giant burrito was the most important thing in the world just then.

"Why don't you guys sit down?" a girl named Daphne asked, although her tone indicated she wasn't too enthusiastic about the prospect. Kelsey always noticed that the girls weren't as friendly to her when Gigi wasn't around.

"Yeah, sit down," Daphne's boyfriend agreed, a little too readily, and Kelsey noticed Daphne's mouth twitch in annoyance.

"Thanks, but we've still got a lot of shopping to do," Kelsey said, trying not to feel too insulted when she noticed the palpable relief on the girls' faces.

Brenden coughed and pulled on Kelsey's sleeve.

"Well, uh, good seeing you guys . . ." She smiled apologetically as they inched their way past the clique's brazen up-and-down stares.

❅   ❅   ❅

When they were out of earshot and seated in a quiet corner with their food trays (a Diet Coke and a grilled cheese sandwich for her, a milkshake and gravy fries for him), Kelsey reached for Brenden's hands underneath the table. "Sorry about that, but if I didn't say hi they'd think I was rude."

Brenden released his hands from hers. "I just don't know why you care so much about what they think of you," he said.

Kelsey's father worked in a machine shop and her family was closer to the poorer side of things than the richer. They lived in a tidy little house off the main road with a front porch and a backyard that faced the woods. It was a decent neighborhood, a little run-down maybe, a little more lower-middle class than middle-middle class. And Brenden lived next door. Their block was certainly nothing like Wade Hill, which was a mile away, up near the mountains, where large, stone, colonial-style manors boasted views of the lake and looked imperiously over the town.

Gigi's father was a successful oncologist at the Cleveland Clinic. It was rumored Gigi had enrolled at Parker only to have a greater chance at getting into Yale because of the geographical quota and the fact that she had no rivals for valedictorian. Her friends who'd prepped at Andover, Exeter, and St. Paul's would face stiff competition.

"They're just a bunch of dumb rich people," Brenden complained, punctuating his sentence by pointing his straw in the air.

"You're wrong, I don't care what they think!" Kelsey protested, stealing a fry from his plate and dipping it in the pool of ketchup. "But I do want to be there for Gigi's birthday."

Gigi could be a bratty pain in the ass sometimes, but she was basically kindhearted. Their freshman year, she had even started a community outreach group to help the town's "less fortunate." Kelsey had joined the after-school club only to die of embarrassment when she found out Gigi had organized a charity food drive to help families in Kelsey's own neighborhood. Kelsey never explained to her parents why there was a basket of canned goods on their porch one afternoon. They ended up donating it to a homeless shelter.

To her credit, Gigi never brought it up, for which Kelsey was glad, and the two girls had forged a real friendship. Kelsey was the only one who knew Gigi's mom had battled alcoholism, and Gigi was always someone fun for Kelsey to gossip with. Most of the time, Gigi bit her tongue about Brenden, who certainly didn't fit into her version of what an "ideal" boyfriend for Kelsey would look like—i.e., preferably one who didn't have grease-stained fingers all the time. Gigi had even innocently inquired once why his parents had spelled his name incorrectly—the proper Irish way was "Brendan." Kelsey had briskly pointed out that their town was full of phonetically spelled first names, like "Kitelynn" (Caitlin) and "Antwone" (Antoine)—not that it had helped her point much.

"The party will be fun, c'mon," Kelsey cajoled in the food court. "I really want to go."

She knew Brenden's reluctance to attend the party stemmed from an incident the past summer. They'd been invited to a Wade Hill picnic by the lake, and Brenden had shown up in a pair of baggy denim cutoffs instead of surfer shorts like the rest of the guys. He was also the only one with two tattoos on his back—a leaping tiger and shamrock. But unlike the Wade Hill preppies, who were baby-soft and pink, regardless of their letterman jackets, Brenden was all tanned sinewy muscle, with a six-pack stomach and protruding hip bones.

"All right." Brenden sighed. "If you want to go, I'll take you."

"You're sure?" she asked keenly. "I don't want to make you do anything you don't want to."

"Do I have a choice?" he joked, raising an eyebrow.

"Not really," she admitted, feeling giddy.

"When have I ever said no to you?" he asked, blushing as she leaned over to kiss him smack on the lips in front of everyone in the food court.

"You won't regret it, I promise," she said. "Especially not when I'm wearing you-know-what."

Now that Brenden had agreed to be her date for the evening—and her mind raced as she wondered how she could convince him to wear something more formal to the event—Kelsey finally allowed herself to be properly excited about Gigi's party. Because for once in her life, she actually had the perfect outfit to wear for the occasion.

In the far reaches of her closet hung a dress carefully concealed in a plastic garment bag, stuffed with tissues and worn only once before. A real Cristóbal Balenciaga gown from the 1960s, made from the finest Parisian silk taffeta, given to her grandmother by the designer himself. A long, long time ago, Kelsey's grandmother had been a model in New York, and had even walked the runways of Paris and Milan.

Kelsey's mom still told stories about how her mother had been discovered by a visiting modeling scout at the bus station, and how she'd left the Midwest for a life of impossible glamour, dating wealthy men twice her age in the big city. Unfortunately, she had gotten pregnant by one of them—a married man, who promptly dumped her and disowned the child she carried. She returned heartbroken to Ohio and died shortly after giving birth to Kelsey's mom.

The year before, Kelsey and her mom were cleaning out the attic when Kelsey came across a dusty old trunk. Inside she found the remaining tokens from her grandmother's short life in the *beau monde*—yellowing magazine clippings of a slim, beautiful blonde whom Kelsey greatly resembled, Stork Club matchbooks, a Pan Am plane ticket to St. Moritz that had never been used. In the bottom of the trunk was a gray plastic garment bag.

"What's this?" she'd asked her mother.

"Oh, I forgot all about it," her mom said wistfully. "It was my mother's and I've been meaning to give it to you one day. Open it."

Inside was a silver silk Balenciaga dress, cut with a dramatic scooped neckline, fitted through the waist, so small and fragile that at first Kelsey was worried it wouldn't fit—but it did, perfectly skimming her figure. The silk was as soft as rose petals. It was almost fifty years old, but the style was clean and classic, there was nothing dowdy or even faintly old-fashioned about it— it was modern, elegant, drop-dead gorgeous. It was her only real heirloom, the one reminder of a grandmother she had never even met.

The Balenciaga dress was the greatest treasure in her closet, and she'd been saving it for a very, very special occasion. She'd modeled it for Brenden in her room several times but had restrained from pulling it out to wear to any of the school dances. Somehow, slow-dancing across the foul lines on the gym's basketball court just didn't seem to do the dress justice.

Gigi McClusky's swanky party, however, felt like the most opportune time to wear it. Everyone in town was breaking their bank accounts to be able to show up in their finest garments, and Kelsey was determined to look just as good.

They finished their meal and Kelsey, still feeling happy about the combined prospect of finally wearing her dress and having Brenden agree to be her date, excused herself to go to the ladies' room.

She was just about to exit her stall when she heard the door open and the clicking of heels on the tile floor. Daphne's and Sarah's voices carried over the sound of the running water and hand-dryers, and Kelsey's ears burned when she realized the Wade Hill girls were talking about . . . her.

"Did you check out the coat? The fur is so fake!"

"She's not fooling anyone with that Kmart special."

Hello, it's from Old Navy, Kelsey thought indignantly.

"I can't WAIT to see what she wears on Saturday!" Sarah whooped, as if Christmas had come early.

"What are you talking about?" a new voice asked, and Kelsey recognized Gigi's level tones.

"Gi!" the girls screamed, as if they'd happened upon a celebrity. "What are you doing here?"

"My mom and I are picking out stuff for the gift bags," Gigi said. "I bumped into the crew at the food court and the guys said you were all in here, as usual. So what's up? What are we discussing?"

"What Kelsey Cooper's going to wear to your party," Sarah informed her.

"Probably that tired black sack she trotted out for Homecoming *and* Fall formals," Daphne snipped. "Don't you think?"

There was an expectant silence. The girls knew Gigi considered Kelsey a friend, and they wondered how she would react to such a nasty breach of etiquette.

Kelsey pressed her ear against the door, just as riveted to hear what her friend would say.

But the silence continued, and for a moment there was no sound but that of Gigi removing the cap from her lip gloss. "I guess," she replied, applying a wand to her practiced pout.

I guess . . .

The words were like a blow . . . even Gigi thought she was a little pathetic for not having new clothes to wear . . . Gigi hadn't even had the heart to defend her . . .

Trapped in the stall, Kelsey's face burned crimson. *I'll show them. I'll show them all.* If they only knew what a prize she had hidden in her closet! The thought of her grandmother's Balenciaga dress was a balm on her wounded pride, but it couldn't take away the hurt she felt at Gigi's betrayal. How could she?

"I really hope she wears those pleather heels again, they're priceless. You know she actually told me they were 'vintage' designer?" Daphne chortled.

"Yeah, I hear that's what they're calling things from the Goodwill these days!"

"Oooh, snap!" Kelsey heard the sound of giggling and of palms slapping high fives.

"Okay, cut it out!" Gigi chastised with a sigh. "Get your claws back in, why don't you? Give the girl a break."

Kelsey's hands were still shaking when she returned to the food court. It was just as she'd suspected—they all saw through her—saw through her discount clothes, the creative thrift-store outfits—they knew she wasn't one of them, and she never would be. They were privileged and pampered, not so much mean but spoiled rotten. They would never understand what it was like to not have everything they ever wanted.

"Hey, what's wrong?" Brenden asked when he saw the look on Kelsey's face.

"Nothing," she said, shaking her head, her eyes blinking rapidly. Damn if she would let those stuck-up bitches make her cry! *The dress, the dress—think about the dress. Think of how no one else at the party will be wearing a real haute couture gown.*

Brenden decided not to push it and they left the food court. Kelsey walked around in a daze until they reached the opposite side of the mall and found themselves in front of Saks Fifth Avenue.

"Let's go in," she said, her eyes lighting up at the elegant display of sumptuous shearling coats and jewel-colored gowns on the mannequins. Saks Fifth was by far the nicest store in the mall, and although Kelsey knew she couldn't afford to buy anything they sold, she loved to browse anyway, getting a contact high from all the fabulous designer merchandise. Maybe it would make her feel better.

Brenden made a face but he followed her inside, slouching in his thin jacket.

Kelsey walked purposefully through the maze of glittering cosmetic counters, ignoring the black-clad salesgirls wielding perfume bottles like spray guns, straight to the shoe salon. *Goodwill indeed!* She browsed through the tempting array of magnificent Italian footwear, her heart beating quickly at the sight of such fashionable abundance. Luxurious crocodile pumps, sexy velvet stilettos, rhinestone-encrusted sandals with dizzying price tags . . .

And then she saw them.

Metallic silver leather strappy sandals, with a spindly wooden heel and skating-rink-size crystals in a vertical pattern from ankle to toe.

Oh, what shoes!

"Look at these!" Kelsey cried, her hands trembling as she picked up the pair and showed them to Brenden.

"What's so great about those shoes?" Brenden asked, hands jammed into his pockets, looking out of place in his gas-station shirt and Levi's among the white leather couches. Brenden claimed that he never really understood her whole obsession with fashion, which he thought was kind of silly since Kelsey looked great in anything. He found fashion intimidating and elitist, a part of Kelsey's life and aspirations that excluded him.

"They're perfect," Kelsey breathed, stroking the sandals with reverence. "They'll match my grandmother's dress perfectly. The silver is the same *exact* shade." No one would ever laugh at her in those shoes—those shoes kicked serious ass—those shoes said, *I am stylish, hear me stomp!* They were a pair of man-killers, defiantly sexy, enviable to the extreme. With these shoes on her feet, the

Wade Hill girls would surely shut up. Even Gigi would be impressed.

"Care to try them on, miss?" a salesman asked, appearing quietly by her side.

"I don't know," she said, shaking her head—try them on? Did she dare? She snuck a peek at the sole for the price tag—nine hundred and fifty dollars. Ouch! Was she even worthy of such decadence? But what could it hurt?

"You look about a six and a half?" the salesman purred. "I'll be right back."

"Okay," Kelsey said, feeling faint. She couldn't believe she was actually going to try them on—that they would be hers if only for a little while.

"Huh," Brenden said, gingerly taking a seat at the edge of the nearest chair and looking as if he would leap up as soon as anyone so much as looked at him the wrong way.

Kelsey sat down beside him, feeling like an impostor. Who was she to try on shoes of such craftsmanship and caliber? She couldn't even afford the tax on those things. Part of her was ready to flee, but before she could, the salesman returned bearing an oversized, elegant shoebox, and knelt in front of her feet. He removed the lid and unwrapped the shoes from the crinkly tissue. The crystals refracted the light in a rainbow of brilliant colors.

Hypnotized, Kelsey removed her worn cowboy boots (bought for five bucks at the Value City thrift store) and peeled off her socks. She folded the hems of her jeans up to the knee and only then did she finally slide her feet onto the soles, wiggling her toes through the soft kidskin leather. She bent down to buckle the tiny little straps.

"What do you think?" she asked, looking up at Brenden, her eyes wide and shining. She straightened up and began walking, the high four-inch heels forcing her to walk with a seductive sway.

She smiled at Brenden—a dazzling, heartbreaking smile that lit up her entire face. There was nothing she wanted so much right then as the jeweled sandals on her feet, and yet at the same time she was fully resigned to the fact that they would never be hers to call her own.

Brenden studied her thoughtfully, and after a long time in which she thought he would never say anything, he clasped his hands tightly together. "I think you look absolutely gorgeous," he said at last. Then he broke his gaze and looked down at the carpet intently, as if the answer to the meaning of life could be found in its plush pile.

Kelsey examined herself in the mirror. What a star-studded entrance to Gigi's party she would make in her Balenciaga dress and these Jimmy Choo shoes! She could picture the jealous looks on her so-called friends' faces. Their jaws would drop with their vape pens. But alas, she might as well have asked for the moon. The shoes were impossible to obtain—a glittering, adored prize that would forever be out of her reach.

"You think so?" she asked, shaking her head. "I'm not so sure."

"Miss?" the salesman queried. "Shall we wrap these up?"

"No, thank you," Kelsey said politely, sitting back on the chair. "They're not for me."

She unbuckled the straps with deliberate, reluctant grace, trying to keep her chin up, but all the while knowing that on Saturday night she would have to pair her grandmother's fabulous dress with her mother's old black pumps, which were too big for her and worn at the heel. Worse, those girls were right—they were made of pleather—"plastic leather."

"Ready?" she asked Brenden, when she could trust herself to speak.

❄   ❄   ❄

A few days later Kelsey was beginning to seriously freak out about Brenden's present. The clock was ticking; tomorrow night was Christmas Eve. She caught a bus back to the mall by herself, determined to pick out something. Her budget hadn't changed— she still had no money of her own to speak of aside from the measly two twenties and a crumpled five. But she couldn't let Christmas come and go without giving him something.

She stood longingly in front of his favorite guitar store, twisting the ends of her sweater nervously, the shrill forced merriment of the piped-in carols making her antsy. She knew Christmas shopping wasn't about how much money you spent. It was about watching the face of someone you loved light up in happiness upon receiving a carefully picked-out present. Gifts didn't have to be expensive to be meaningful. But nevertheless she wished forty-five dollars bought something more substantial than a gift certificate at Radio Shack.

"Kelsey!"

She turned around. Gigi was bearing down on her, holding aloft her signature venti cup of soy-milk mochaccino and a dozen overstuffed shopping bags from a variety of expensive boutiques.

"Oh, hi," Kelsey said, trying to muster the usual enthusiasm. She still hadn't quite forgiven her friend for what she'd overheard the other afternoon. Although technically, Gigi hadn't done anything wrong—she *had* asked the girls to quit it—albeit *after* they had already raked Kelsey over the fashion coals. Gigi's lukewarm "I guess" wasn't exactly a stab in the back, but Kelsey felt like asking "Et tu, Brute?" just the same.

"You okay?" Gigi asked, smiling nervously, picking up on Kelsey's aloof manner.

Kelsey shrugged. "I can't seem to find anything for Brenden for Christmas," she admitted, although she would rather drink a gallon of her dad's gross eggnog before she ever confessed she was looking for a gift in the under-forty-five-dollar range.

"Totally! Boys are so hard to shop for," Gigi sympathized, smiling broadly. "I can't find anything for Jared either. I've been so bad! All I'm doing is buying stuff for myself. They have the cutest things at J. Crew—wanna go see? Maybe you'll find something for Brenden there."

Kelsey had no choice. She had to hang out with Gigi now, and give up the perfect-gift quest momentarily. Her friend dragged her from store to store, from Topshop to Zara, and with a sinking heart, Kelsey found herself inside the shoe salon at Saks Fifth Avenue once again.

Gigi tossed her bags on the ground and began barking orders to the scurrying salesmen, who hurried to keep up with her.

Kelsey walked over to the familiar display and found her beloved sandals on a Lucite pedestal. They were just as beautiful as she remembered.

"*Those* are cute!" Gigi said, suddenly appearing by her side and scooping up the pair. "Can I get these in a six and a half?" she called to the nearest salesman. "For my party?" she asked Kelsey. "Don't you think?"

Kelsey's stomach dropped. Gigi probably wouldn't even wear them. She'd already told Kelsey how she'd picked out a sweet pair of the latest platform heels to wear with her dress when her family was in Chicago the other month. The thought of her precious shoes ending up in the bottom of Gigi's closet was almost too much for Kelsey to bear.

But the owl-faced salesman came back with a frown. "We're out of the six and a half, ma'am. I believe I sold the last pair this morning. I'm sorry."

Gigi grimaced. "Oh, well. I'll just take these Pradas then," she said, thrusting several pairs of shoeboxes at the guy.

Kelsey exhaled.

❋   ❋   ❋

That evening, Brenden came over, and they took a walk through the woods behind their houses to look over the ravine. The jagged edge of the sloping cliff opened up to a true wilderness. Growing up, they had chased each other through the forest of trees, falling over logs, collecting frogs, catching poison ivy. Every winter since Kelsey could remember they went sledding down the hill that ran by the frozen creek and afterward her mom would make them hot chocolate with puffy marshmallows on top.

"You've been quiet lately. What's up?" Brenden asked. He himself appeared jumpy and excited, on the verge of telling her something, but then he would bite his lip and look away.

Kelsey shook her head and inhaled deeply. The air was tinged with just a slight edge of burning firewood—a pleasant, smoky aroma that she always associated with Christmas. The moon shone above them, barely a crescent, before disappearing into the clouds.

"C'mon, babe, talk to me," Brenden said, putting his arms around her and leaning his head on her shoulder. Usually it was Kelsey who tried to draw Brenden out of his shell, but not this time.

"I was just thinking . . ." She sighed. Thinking of Gigi's upcoming party, and all the anxieties that it had wrought—the dress, the shoes, the myriad disappointments before she had even stepped one foot inside the heated tents. Part of her wanted to be done with it.

Brenden rubbed his hands up and down the back of her coat, and she ran her fingers through his thick dark hair. He would be so handsome if he just wore it back, so that everyone could see his face—his sculpted, aquiline nose, and his deep, chameleon blue-green eyes. Eyes that were looking at her intently, as if trying to guess the secret behind her sorrowful mood.

They stood silently for a long time, just holding each other.

"Whatever it is that's bothering you, I'm sure everything's going to turn out all right," Brenden said gently. "It's Christmas after all."

"You're right, it's not important." She pressed against him, and they started with just baby kisses, a kiss on the forehead, the nose, the chin, and then she opened her mouth to his, and they kissed, with a growing passion, until his hands were no longer on top of her coat but underneath it, and up the back of her shirt. His palms rested flat against the small of her back, and she had dug her own hands underneath his denim jacket, inside his flannel shirt, and still they were kissing, and then he was kissing her neck, her clavicles, so softly that each kiss felt like a dance of butterflies against her skin.

Brenden buried his face in her neck and she hugged him tightly, suddenly noticing how much he was shaking from the cold underneath his thin denim jacket.

And that's when she knew.

She knew exactly what she was going to get him for Christmas, but more important, she knew exactly how she would be able to afford it.

Her hands suddenly felt clammy and cold, knowing the sacrifice she would soon have to make.

❄   ❄   ❄

Christmas Eve morning shone clear and bright, and in her bed-room Kelsey was standing in front of her closet, contemplating a gray plastic garment bag.

Last night she'd made her decision.

The black leather motorcycle jacket. It was perfect—Brenden would look so kickass in it, riding on his Harley. It was tough, authentic, and well made. Kelsey was sure he would love it as much as his bike. She'd seen the way he'd looked at it at the store when he'd come in to buy replacement grips for his handlebars. It would keep him warm, and it was just his style. She couldn't imagine him wearing anything else on the back of his bike. He would keep it forever, and would think about her every time he wore it, which would be every day, she was sure.

But the jacket cost four hundred dollars, when she only had forty-five.

Kelsey unzipped the garment bag slowly, taking out her grand-mother's Balenciaga dress so she could see it shine in the light.

She caressed the whisper-soft fabric, the handmade label signed by the master himself. She was too practical a girl to regret never having worn it now. It was the only way. There were a bunch of vintage stores in downtown Cleveland, the city was famous for them—stylists from Hollywood and New York rou-tinely made the rounds to cull the racks for the most fabulous vintage finds. She'd heard of vintage Pucci dresses selling for thousands of dollars, of Oscar starlets wearing 1950s Ossie Clark jersey dresses bought in Cleveland. What would they pay for a real, vintage Cristóbal Balenciaga?

Well, she would just have to find out.

She quickly stowed the dress back in the bag, zipped it up, and walked out of her bedroom before she could change her mind. Downstairs, her mother was standing in the kitchen, making Christmas cookies with Kelsey's younger sister, Haley, who was eight.

"Hi, sweetheart. Want to help us make thumbprints?" her mother asked, her cheeks white with flour.

"Maybe later. Does Dad need the car?"

"No, he's sleeping. He worked late last night and he's off today, for once. It is Christmas Eve, after all."

"Cool, can I borrow it?" Kelsey asked, trembling slightly. If her mom said no, or if the car was out of gas or something, she wasn't sure if she could go through with it. She wasn't that brave.

"Sure, honey." Her mother nodded.

"I'll be out for a while, but I'll be back before dinner," Kelsey said, taking the keys from the basket by the door.

"Aren't you going to Gigi's party tonight?"

"Uh-huh," Kelsey called over her shoulder. "Brenden's taking me."

She drove quickly on newly plowed roads—there had been a snowstorm the night before, and the highway was slick and wet from salting. Her heart beat fast in her chest. There was an elegant vintage resale shop in the Coventry district, a neighborhood dotted with cool record stores and cute French bistros. She'd been there several times before, and she knew the proprietress had an eye for designer dresses.

Kelsey parked the car by a snowbank and entered the cozy warmth of the shop, the garment bag draped over one shoulder.

"Hi," she said shyly to the stern-looking woman behind the glass counter. "Do you, uh, buy vintage clothes here?"

"Only if they are worthwhile," the owner said in a frosty voice. She looked at Kelsey, taking in the bargain coat, the jeans, the scuffed cowboy boots.

"Well, I have something of my grandmother's. I don't know, but I think it could be worth something." She laid the garment bag on the counter and unzipped it, removing the dress from its tissued environment. "It's a Balenciaga, from the sixties. It's only been worn once, I think. She got it in Paris."

The shopkeeper put on a pair of half-moon spectacles, and regarded the dress silently. Her wrinkled hands caressed the soft fabric. "My goodness."

"It's nice, isn't it?"

"How much do you want for it?" the owner asked sharply.

Kelsey was at a loss. She had never considered naming a price. She'd just thought it would be worth something—but what? She shrugged. "How much would you give me for it?"

"Three hundred."

Kelsey tried not to look too excited. Three hundred dollars! But then she remembered: The motorcycle jacket was four hundred. She noticed a few gowns hanging by the rack. One of them read HALSTON, 1975, $565.

"Six hundred," she countered, looking the woman in the eye.

"Four," the owner said.

"Five."

"Four-fifty, and that's my final offer."

Then the deal was done, and Kelsey walked out of the shop, clutching in her hand four one-hundred dollar bills, two twenties, and a ten. She'd done it.

She got into her car, shut the door, and blinked back tears. This was stupid, she thought. She'd *wanted* to sell it. She was doing it for Brenden. Her heart leaped when she thought of how he would smile when she saw his brand-new leather jacket! She drove straight to the Harley-Davidson store; she had to get there soon since it would probably close early for Christmas Eve.

A few hours later, inside her bedroom, Kelsey looked at herself in the mirror that hung over the door. The Wade Hill girls were certainly going to have a field day. She was wearing the same black dress she'd worn several times already. It was a simple, serviceable, average, black wool crepe with a square neckline, spaghetti straps. She'd purchased it on sale at the Gap for a fraction of its original price. She brushed her hair back until it shone, and carefully applied her makeup.

She took a step back from the mirror, assessing her reflection. She knew Brenden would be looking forward to seeing her in the silver Balenciaga. Would he be disappointed if he saw her in the same old dress? Would he still think she was the prettiest girl in the room? Next to the Wade Hill peacocks and all their new and expensive finery?

Kelsey clipped on her earrings—gold-tone hoops—and attempted a smile. So what if she was wearing the same old thing? There would be no grand entrance at the party, no star-making turn. She would just be one of the girls in the background. She chided herself for her girlish vanity; it was Gigi's birthday party, after all, not hers. Why had she been so obsessed with making a splash?

"Sweetheart, Brenden's here," her mother singsonged from downstairs.

She took a final pirouette, pulled up on the bustline to make sure it stayed in place, and then walked downstairs. The Coopers' living room had been richly decorated for Christmas—pine needles were scattered on the mantel, and the tree shone with multicolored lights, decorated with the handmade ornaments she and her sister had made in a succession of art classes—a wooden carved teddy bear with her name on it, Haley's handprint from kindergarten.

The fireplace was crackling, throwing off red sparks, and the house was warm and inviting. Brenden was waiting for her at the bottom of the staircase.

For a moment, Kelsey wasn't sure what she was seeing. "Bren—you're in a tie!" she exclaimed. "And your hair!" She almost tripped on the final step in her excitement.

She couldn't believe it. Brenden was wearing a proper sport coat and a dark tie. Gone were his dirty, grease-stained jeans and his ragged T-shirts. There wasn't a black armband in sight. He had even combed his long hair back, just like she'd always wanted him to, and she was right—without the hair in his eyes, he was even more incredibly handsome. Now everyone would notice, not just her. But why was he looking at her with that peculiar expression on his face?

"What's up?" he asked, holding a corsage in a plastic container and another package under his arm. "Where's your grandmother's dress?"

Kelsey pretended not to hear him. "I thought ties made you claustrophobic," she said flirtatiously, walking toward him, her fingers reaching out to brush his lapel.

"Yeah, well." He shrugged, trying to look nonchalant about his makeover. "But what's going on? Why aren't you wearing you-know-what?"

"Oh, that old thing." Kelsey tried to affect a careless laugh. "Forget about it. It's so old-fashioned, really, don't you think?" She kept talking, babbling, to cover up for her distress. He *was* disappointed. He kept looking at her with that strange, curious, blank expression on his face.

"What's wrong with this dress?" she asked a bit fiercely. "Don't you like how I look?"

"No—no. You look beautiful in whatever you wear, you know that, it's just . . ." Brenden shrugged his shoulders helplessly.

"Wait! I want to give you something. Hold on." Kelsey took the stairs two at a time and returned bearing a large white box with the Harley-Davidson symbol on it.

"Merry Christmas!" she said cheerfully. "C'mon, open it. Don't just stand there looking at it." She pulled him over to the couch and balanced the box carefully on his knees. Brenden put aside the corsage and his present for now.

He was speechless and stared at the box with trepidation, as if willing for the black-and-orange logo to transform into something else. Finally, he lifted the lid.

"It's the jacket you wanted!" Kelsey exclaimed. "See? Put it on! Let's see how it looks." She helped him take off his sport coat. "Now you can ride your Harley in style! And it's sooo warm. The guy at the shop said it's lined in sheepskin." Brenden nodded, putting on the motorcycle jacket.

"It looks fantastic!" Kelsey declared. She was right—he looked just like James Dean in it—or was it Marlon Brando? One of those old movie stars in those 1950s films that her mom sometimes watched. She bubbled over with happiness at how good her boyfriend looked in her gift. It was worth the sacrifice. Although she still couldn't get over how incredibly stunned he seemed—almost as if he were blindsided by her gift. Not quite the reaction she had expected.

"Don't you like it, Bren?" she asked, her voice quavering.

He finally spoke, and his features relaxed into his quick smile. "Of course I love it. It's from you," he said as he began to take off the jacket. He placed it gently on the couch next to him. "But here, I got this for you. So you could wear it to the party tonight." He handed her a silver box, wrapped in the signature Saks Fifth Avenue holiday paper—silver with red ribbon. "Merry Christmas, Kelsey."

"Oh, my God," Kelsey said, sinking back on the couch, not quite sure if she had the right to hope what she was hoping. "You *didn't*!"

Brenden smiled, leaning back on the couch and making himself comfortable.

"No way, no way!" she exclaimed as she ripped open the paper and opened the lid. But yes. There they were. She put her hands to her mouth, and tears sprang to her eyes, threatening to smudge her mascara. Brenden had bought them for her. She felt dizzy with shock. How had he been able to afford them? The cherished metallic silver sandals—the crystal disks glowing in the box like diamonds. Gorgeous, and finally hers. The last pair in size six and a half. Her heart quickened to a frantic pulse. This was unbelievable, this was the best Christmas ever. Nothing had prepared her for this . . .

"Oh, my god, Brenden. How . . . ?" she whispered, placing the lid back on the box and stroking it affectionately.

"Go on now, go change into that Balen-whatever dress and put 'em on," he urged, his eyes shining with delight. "Let's see how they look together."

Her grandmother's dress! The Balenciaga! In the excitement of the moment she had completely forgotten that it was no longer hers to wear with the silvery shoes. Utterly miserable and devastated, Kelsey was afraid to meet her boyfriend's eye. In the smallest voice she could muster, she finally confessed. "I sold the dress to buy you the jacket."

"You . . ." Brenden said, trying not to look too alarmed.

"But don't worry, Bren—I can get it back, I can get on a payment plan with the boutique—once I have enough babysitting money . . ." Her voice trailed off hopelessly. The dress was gone forever—they both knew that.

He nodded slowly in comprehension, and rubbed his chin thoughtfully.

"But see, they look good with this dress, too!" Kelsey said, slipping off her mom's old heels and sliding into the precious stilettos. All right, so it didn't quite have the same effect as it would have had with the Balenciaga dress, but the shoes were still stunning.

She jumped off the couch and pulled him up. "I know it's cold, but it's not a long ride up to the party. Do you have my helmet? Let's get on the Harley and go. I don't want to miss

Gigi's grand entrance!" she added gaily. "Put on your new jacket now, c'mon!"

Brenden let her help him back into his new black leather jacket and they made their way to the front door. Kelsey flung it open and was flummoxed to find the street empty. Brenden usually parked his Harley right in front of his driveway next door.

"Where's the Hog?" she asked, looking around wildly. Slowly, she began to understand what he had done. *No.* She didn't deserve it. She didn't deserve him . . .

"Babe," Brenden said, pulling her close and kissing her cheek, so she could feel his stubble. "I sold the bike to buy you the shoes."

He smiled at her, pushing a stray lock of hair back behind her ear. "We've got to take my mom's Dodge Shadow," he said, motioning to the rusty clunker hunkered on the street with the 1980s-style pastel brush marks on the side.

Brenden, still wearing his tough biker jacket, wrenched open the passenger door to the decades-old compact car and Kelsey climbed inside.

Whatever would people say once they arrived at the party?

Then Kelsey realized with a laugh that she couldn't care less what anyone thought—of her dress, her shoes, or her boyfriend. Especially what they thought of her boyfriend.

That Christmas, she had received a gift more precious than anything a designer could ever offer or sell. A gift that was truly priceless. A gift akin to those that the magi gave on Christmas Eve. She had received the gift of Brenden's heart. And even better yet, she had given her heart openly to him—and for that, she felt such an immense swell of happiness it seemed as if her heart would burst from joy.

Brenden turned the key and winked at Kelsey as the engine sputtered to life. "What do you think?" he asked, reaching over to squeeze her hand. "We're a pair of crazy kids, huh?"

The Dodge Shadow inched its way forward in the snow, the tire chains scrunching on the gravelly road. It was freezing outside, and the car's heater hadn't worked since 1989, but neither of them were cold.

GROUNDED

BY NIC STONE

Tfw you finally understand that whole busted camel hump/straw saying . . .

Umm. Whut?

The sayiiiiiiiing! The straw that busted the camel hump?

. . .

"The straw that broke the camel's back"?

YOU KNEW WHAT I MEANT STOP BEING A SMARTASS.

Heh.

What are we talking about again?

I, Leigh Danielle Wells, am a camel and my back/hump/WHATEVER has been broken/busted/WHATEVER by a final straw.

Ah. And what straw is that?

Actually, what are any of the straws?

Where did the straws come from?

Are they long straws?

Short?

Flexi?

The lil red ones you stir coffee with?

You really get on my nerves sometimes, Niecey.

At your service, Madame.

So you gonna tell me about the straws?

Wait, how are you even texting me?

Aren't you in the air right now?

Can you text from the air?

Been awhile since I was on a plane . . .

I'm not in the air. Which is one of the straws.

Go on.

Well my flight got canceled. ALL flights into AND out of Atlanta have been grounded.

Oh. Dang.

Yeah.

Fight to get out of Massachusetts only to get stuck here.

But it's Christmas Eeeeeeeeve!

No poop, Poirot.

. . .

You lost me on that one, Champ.

Oh come on! Hercule Poirot?

Agatha Christie's most famous and skillful detective?

Let's . . . just get back to the matter at hand.

Will you make it out before 11 p.m.?

ATL to Palm Beach can't be THAT long a flight . . .

Whatever.

And doubtful. It's sleeting here. Apparently Atlanta's kind of a punk when it comes to "winter weather" as the advisory on the news is calling it.

Makes sense I guess.

So straw one = canceled flight?

No. Straw one = Chrismukah in friggin Florida.

And fine, the "ukah" part is technically over, but we always do something to celebrate anyway . . .

Except now we probably won't because the Kemps aren't Jewish.

Speaking of which . . .

I know we've been friends since freshman year but . . .

It's still weird to me that YOU are actually Jewish.

You know, being black and all.

#GetYouAGirlWhoCanDoBoth

Speaking of which, my bubbe said thanks again for the cornbread recipe.

Awww! I love Mama Olga so much.

Kinda wish I had a Russian/Jewish grandma

Another straw: I'm not even gonna get to see her.

God, of all the places to spend the WINTER holidays.

CHRISMUKAH IS SUPPOSED TO BE FRIGID AND SNOWY SO EVERYONE STAYS INSIDE BY THE FIRE!

Florida? Palm BEACH, even?

SERIOUSLY?

flips table

And you can't even get there.

#Grounded

EXACTLY!

So which one broke your hump?

Huh?

We've got three straws so far:

1. Winter holidays in Florida

2. No Bubbe

3. Canceled flight . . .

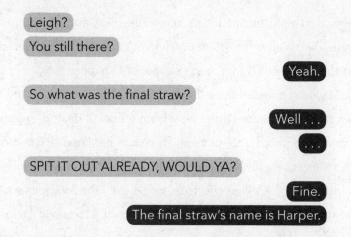

Leigh?

You still there?

Yeah.

So what was the final straw?

Well . . .

. . .

SPIT IT OUT ALREADY, WOULD YA?

Fine.

The final straw's name is Harper.

Leigh Wells drops her phone into her lap and crosses her arms. Huffs. Never in her life did she expect to hate the sound of Christmas music.

Her eyes scan the ceiling of gate C42 in the heart of the Atlanta airport, hunting—like a hangry hawk, she feels—for the source of what's usually one of her favorite holiday tunes: Pentatonix's "White Winter Hymnal."

When she spots the speaker, she growls. Like . . . aloud. The white-haired, white-skinned woman sitting next to Leigh shoots her some serious side-eye before swiftly gathering her belongings and relocating to a different seat.

Leigh can't help but growl, though. It's Christmas friggin Eve and she's trapped in an airport. And that's after getting trapped at the super snooty boarding school she attends in western Massachusetts for three *days* of an already too-short winter break. A massive snowstorm had the whole school locked down, and

Leigh narrowly escaped this morning—just to get re-stuck. Again, due to snow. In Atlanta. Where it's supposed to be warmer and these types of things aren't supposed to happen.

Maybe she jinxed herself. Her personal preference would've been to slide a hundred miles west from school to Boston—home. In truth, she really doesn't *want* to reach her final destination. Who wants to spend Christmas in hot/sunny Palm Beach, Florida?

Still though: When the voice came over the loudspeaker to announce that "All flights into and out of Hartsfield-Jackson International Airport" (which, according to a sign she saw, is the "busiest airport in the world") "have been grounded due to accumulating ice and snow here in Atlanta," a sour taste filled Leigh's mouth and she immediately wanted to throw something.

Now the Christmas music sounds like violence-filled noise and she feels personally attacked by the onslaught of wreaths and holly and Christmas trees and twinkling lights strung up friggin *everywhere*.

On top of all THAT, precisely thirteen minutes after the grounding announcement, her phone buzzed. And THAT, as she's told her best friend, Niecey, was the final straw, busting Leigh's hump all to pieces.

Frankly, it *shouldn't* be that big a deal, getting an innocuous pair of text messages from Harper Kemp. Yeah, it's been three years since the girls have seen each other, and yeah, they're about to inhabit the same space in Palm Beach for a solid seven days, nine hours, and thirty-two minutes—Leigh did the math the minute Mama and Daddy smacked her with the news that they'd be spending Christmas through New Year's Day at the home of Janice and Kwame Kemp, their best friends from college.

But it clearly *is* a big deal if Leigh's heart is racing the way it does just before she reads a new piece of poetry at an open mic night. Like some part of her soul is about to be on display and people can throw whatever they want at it.

Which is so dumb. They're *texts*.

Right?

Leigh taps back over to the messages from a number with no name attached.

> Leigh? This is Harper.
> Kemp.

Leigh would've known it was Harper *Kemp* without the second message—ten minutes before she got the messages, she was on the phone with Mama, who'd let her know *Oh hey, sweetheart, Harper's stuck in Atlanta too. Her flight was earlier than yours but also got canceled. I gave Janice your number to pass along to Harper, so she'll probably reach out. Maybe the two of you can wait things out together.*

And even without *that* Leigh would've known.

There's only one Harper.

And now it's been twenty-seven minutes since Harper sent Leigh those messages.

So what do I say, Niecey?

It's been almost a half hour!

You're such a drama queen, Leigh.

Maybe start with "Hi!"?

UGH, I just . . .

Fine.

Leigh takes a deep breath . . .

Harper! Hi!

Sorry for the delay . . .

My phone was on silent.

(She has no clue why she's lying.)

No prob!

Long time no see, huh? ☺

I know, right?

What's it been, three years?

Crazy . . .

Sorry for texting out of the blue.

Moms gave me your number, and I figured since we're both stuck here . . .

Maybe we could link up?

Would that be cool?

Crap.

Leigh switches back over to Niecey:

> She wants to link up, Nieceyyyy!

Umm . . . were you expecting something else?

> WHAT DO I SAY NOW?

"Okay" would suffice?

> But what if it's awkward?
> I haven't seen her since we were 14.

Okay . . . and?

You're about to spend a week with her, L.

Like . . . in her HOUSE.

> DON'T REMIND ME!

Might wanna start getting reacquainted . . .

WHY are you being weird about this?

Who even is this person?

Except that's a question Leigh doesn't really know how to answer.

Well, okay, that's not entirely true. Leigh *could* tell Niecey about how the last time Leigh and Harper saw each other—joint family cruise to the Bahamas the summer before ninth grade— things got weird on the last day.

Well, at least for Leigh they did.

She and Harper had been at the on-boat pool together (still so weird to think about: a pool on a vessel in the middle of the ocean), and it was time to go get ready for the final dinner of the trip.

Which was fine. They'd been in the water for a solid three hours at that point and Leigh's fingers and toes were all gross and pruney. Also, her hair—typically big and curly, but presently crispy as burnt rotini noodles—was gonna give Mama a conniption, because Leigh hadn't worn her swim cap like she was supposed to.

It was truly time to get out.

Except Harper did first.

And when she did, Leigh noticed.

It was the stomach that caught her attention. Harper's stomach was smooth and brown, the color of roasted almonds, faintly lined with muscles that flexed beneath her skin as she pushed herself out of the pool and stood upright.

Then the legs.

Long. Lean. Again with the flexing muscles.

And Leigh felt super weird about it, but the addition of dripping water to those otherwise regular ol' body parts . . .

Well.

It was confusing.

And the weirdest part was no matter how hard she tried—and she *really* did try—Leigh couldn't seem to pull her eyes away.

She eventually heard her name in Mama's voice. And when Leigh's eyes snapped up to Harper's face, Harper's furrowed brow and narrowed eyes made it *crystal* clear she'd caught Leigh staring.

In that exact moment, Mama walked up wagging her finger and fussing, and Leigh had never been more grateful. Harper took it as her cue to exit with nothing more than an "Uhh, see ya!" And Leigh pretty much hid in the cabin for the rest of the cruise.

Barring the awkward wave they exchanged as the Wellses and Kemps went their separate ways upon getting off the boat, *that* was the last time the girls had seen each other.

And maybe Harper doesn't even remember, Leigh tells herself. She and Harper were having a great time together on that cruise before the whole thing, and they've each been through seven semesters of high school since, so maybe the incident got blotted out of Harper's memory by a combination of elapsed time and new experiences.

Leigh reads back through Harper's texts. They seem pretty innocuous. Distinctly *not* laced with uncomfortable recollections of being ogled by another girl . . .

Leigh is probably overthinking this.

Right?

She lays her phone facedown in her lap and lets her gaze drift out the window. The snow is really coming down now. It's actually kinda pretty.

Maybe this is exactly what Leigh needed: to get grounded. Literally and otherwise. The past couple of months have been . . . trying. The breakup with Jabari definitely took a toll—largely because "Lebari," as everyone referred to them, was considered *the* premier senior couple at the Evanscroft School of Northampton, MA. So for the first few weeks, it seemed like the entire school was grieving. For the first *week*, in fact, every time Leigh came back to her dorm, there was a new pile of sympathy gifts: flowers, expensive candy, stuffed animals. There was even a Louis Vuitton clutch with a flask hidden inside on day three.

Interestingly enough though, the breakup itself wasn't the main thing on Leigh's mind.

That's what she hasn't mustered up the courage to tell Niecey: the *real* reason "Lebari" fell apart.

Because while Harper was the first girl Leigh ever noticed in *that* way, she certainly isn't the last.

Nor the most recent.

And frankly, Leigh doesn't know what to do with that. Everyone thinks there's some big, ugly secret behind the breakup, but in truth, Leigh just . . . stopped being interested in Jabari.

Actually that's not quite true. It's more like Leigh started to realize she'd never been into him in the first place. And *that* only happened because of Zuri, a transfer student from Kenya who was by far the most beautiful girl Leigh had ever seen. Leigh's mind would go blank and her palms would get sweaty whenever Zuri was in the same room. And when Leigh started thinking—and dreaming—about Zuri in ways she'd *never* thought about Jabari . . .

Yeah.

She tried to hold on, Leigh did. Went so far as to sometimes*
(*always) shut her eyes whenever it was possible to take a moment
and imagine that Jabari was Zuri whenever she was with him
(even/especially when they were making out).

He eventually noticed something was off.

They parted amicably.

And while Leigh knows no one would take issue with her lik-
ing girls, the whole thing—the completely undeniable *shift*—was
disorienting.

So disorienting, Leigh hasn't even been able to tell her best-
friend-since-ninth-grade the truth.

One thing Niecey's right about though: Leigh *is* about to
spend a week with Harper Kemp, and there's no way she'll be
able to avoid her the whole time.

So . . .

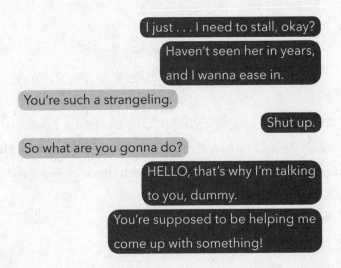

I just . . . I need to stall, okay?

Haven't seen her in years,
and I wanna ease in.

You're such a strangeling.

Shut up.

So what are you gonna do?

HELLO, that's why I'm talking
to you, dummy.

You're supposed to be helping me
come up with something!

You're ridiculous.

But fine.

Mmmmmm . . .

What about some kind of game?

Game?

Yeah.

You're trapped in an airport, right?

Airports are cool.

Have some fun with it.

Okay . . .

How?

I dunno!

Maybe some kinda cat and
mouse type thing?

Cat and mouse . . .

Yes, jackass.

Like she has to find you.

And you can like give her clues from
your surroundings or something.

Which triggers a different set of memories for Leigh—of all the stuff she and Harper did *before* the pool incident: the Hide-and-Seek and I Spy and talking to each other in code over the walkie-talkies Harper's dad gave them.

And then she's got it.

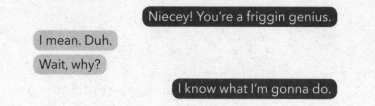

Niecey! You're a friggin genius.

I mean. Duh.

Wait, why?

I know what I'm gonna do.

After grabbing all her stuff, Leigh leaves the gate area in a rush. She heads toward the escalator that will take her down to the "Plane Train"—Atlanta airport's mode of transportation between the six concourses that house all the flight gates for people who don't want/aren't able to walk.

Three stops to concourse T, then out and up the escalator.

As soon as she's at the top, Leigh pulls her phone out and takes a deep breath. Taps to the right set of messages.

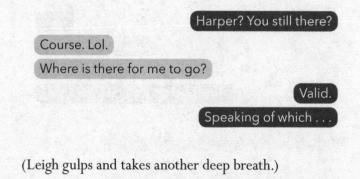

Harper? You still there?

Course. Lol.

Where is there for me to go?

Valid.

Speaking of which . . .

(Leigh gulps and takes another deep breath.)

Remember that cruise we went on with the parentals when we were 14?

How could I forget?

☺

(Leigh's not entirely sure what to do with that, but . . .)

Well . . . and this is probably super corny?

But remember the games we
played? Like, I Spy . . .

Hide and Seek.

Secret Agent . . .

Yo, you remember those walkies
my dad gave us to play with??

(Leigh is blown away right now.)

I do!

Would you uhh . . .

Wanna play a game like that?

Since we're stuck here and all . . .

☺

What'd you have in mind, Miss Leigh?

It takes Leigh all of thirty seconds to figure out the first clue.

❊　　❊　　❊

198

"Wait, you're really doing it?!" comes Niecey's voice over Leigh's headphones. As soon as Harper said yes to Leigh's game proposal, Leigh tapped away from messages to call her best friend.

"Yeah," Leigh replies. "You thought I was joking?"

"I mean . . . ish? I knew you were semi-serious cuz I know how busybody-esque you get when you're all panicked . . . but I didn't expect you to take *my* advice. You literally never do."

"Well, if we're being honest, Niece, your advice is pretty trash most of the time."

"Hey now!"

"You know I'm right." Leigh looks around for a terminal landmark of some sort to include in the rhyming text hint she's planning to send to Harper as soon as she gets back down to Plane Train level. "Remember that time you suggested I pour maple syrup in Kennedy Moscovich's gym bag because *you* claimed she was flirting with Jabari?"

"Whatever. I know what I saw."

"Still." Leigh's eyes alight on a currency exchange booth located across the main concourse from the clue she's chosen: a family of six, including a fat baby, all decked out in matching flannel shirts, dog-piled on the floor near the back wall of gate area T6. She smiles.

"So what exactly are you doing?" Niecey asks

"Well, it's sort of an I Spy meets Hide-and-Seek scavenger hunt?"

"*So* extra, Leigh."

"Shut it. So I'm going through the terminals looking for stuff I can send her a 'hint' about, and then she has to go find the thing and text me a picture of it."

"That actually sounds kinda fun."

"It *does*, doesn't it?"

"What's the endgame though?"

Leigh steps onto the escalator, and as she descends, she gets smacked with a wave of shaky nerves. She'd told Harper to stay put until she receives the first set of instructions, but what if Harper didn't listen and is headed this way and they run into each other before Leigh's ready—

"Leigh? You there?"

"Yeah, yeah. I'm here."

"So . . . endgame? You plan to send her on a wild-goose chase for how long exactly?"

"It's not a wild-goose chase."

"Oh it isn't?"

Leigh huffs. "Look, I need to stall until we've gotten reacquainted by text." Which definitely wasn't Leigh's initial intention (*run away for as long as possible* was), but she guesses it makes sense now that she's said it aloud. "Obviously I'll have to actually see her *here* at the airport eventually, I just . . . need a little time."

"Hmm," Niecey replies. "You still haven't told me what the deal is with this girl, and I'm not buying that *we haven't seen each other in years* nonsense. BUT, I'm interested in hearing how this whole game thing goes, so I'll let you slide. For now."

Leigh walks past the train platform and into the long tunnel with moving sidewalks that leads from the T-gates to concourse A. She smiles. There's something very freeing about not getting on the train. About moving at her own pace and actually taking the time to absorb her surroundings.

When was the last time she'd done that?

"I gotta go," she tells Niecey as she spots what she's instantly knows will be the second clue.

"Yeah, okay," Niecey says. "Keep me posted."

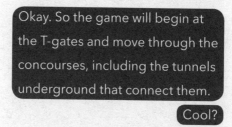

So you ready, Harper?

I was born ready, homegirl.
☺

(That makes Leigh smile.)

Okay. So the game will begin at the T-gates and move through the concourses, including the tunnels underground that connect them.

Cool?

With it.

You can take the Plane Train to the T-gates.

Got it.

Okay, first hint:

Across from where Brits change their pounds, a plaid-clad pack of peeps abounds. See them slumber cute and cozy. Find the one whose cheeks are rosy.

Wow, Leigh.

You certainly know how to turn a phrase.

That was tight.

(Leigh's sure glad her skin is brown because *her* cheeks would be rosy right now otherwise.)

Thank you.

You're welcome.

Headed down to the train now.

I'm pretty excited.

Leigh smiles again.

Yeah.

So am I.

❀   ❀   ❀

By the time Leigh's phone buzzes again, she's on her way back down to the between-concourse tunnels after figuring out what clue number three will be. (She's really proud of this one, and is almost sure it will make Harper smile . . . something she didn't realize she cared about until this moment).

When she opens the text, there's a photo of the flannel family: Dad is awake now and reading a book, but the cute, fat baby—whom Harper digitally circled in the picture—is still sound asleep, mouth wide, on the mom's chest.

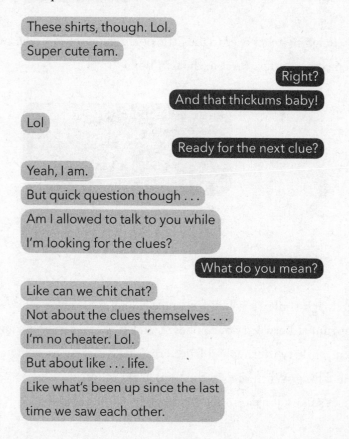

These shirts, though. Lol.

Super cute fam.

Right?

And that thickums baby!

Lol

Ready for the next clue?

Yeah, I am.

But quick question though . . .

Am I allowed to talk to you while I'm looking for the clues?

What do you mean?

Like can we chit chat?

Not about the clues themselves . . .

I'm no cheater. Lol.

But about like . . . life.

Like what's been up since the last time we saw each other.

Oh.

(Well, that was unexpected . . .)

Of course we can talk.

Cool, cool.

So . . .

Wait, what's the next hint? Lol.

Oh duh. My bad.

Leigh switches over to the little poem she wrote for clue two, then copies and pastes it in the text box:

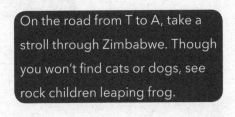

On the road from T to A, take a stroll through Zimbabwe. Though you won't find cats or dogs, see rock children leaping frog.

Nice!

😊

I'm on it.

Leigh smiles—which feels nice—and approaches the walking tunnel between concourses A and B. She hears the sounds first: birds twittering and frogs croaking, crickets creaking and rain falling. When she *sees* the tunnel, she stops.

It's like a jungle. Inside the airport.

The ceiling is covered in what look like metal sheets, cut to resemble a tree canopy. Said sheets are backlit by different shades of green, blue, and purple light. There are also blinking yellow lights that simulate the appearance of fireflies, and lights that "splash" on the floor to mimic raindrops.

Leigh is mesmerized.

And then her phone buzzes.

The message contains a picture of a sculpture featuring four children in the thick of play: Three are lined up and bent at the waist with their hands on their knees, and the fourth is using his hands to launch himself up and over the middle kid's back.

Man, these sculptures are incredible

I didn't even know this was down here!

Which is shameful considering how often I use this airport.

I always just take the train.

Smh.

I mean for what it's worth . . .

I only found the stuff down here because we started this game.

Speaking of which, wait til you get to the location of clue 4.

I'm standing here now, and you're basically gonna die.

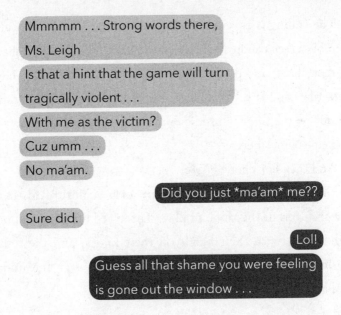

Mmmmm . . . Strong words there, Ms. Leigh

Is that a hint that the game will turn tragically violent . . .

With me as the victim?

Cuz umm . . .

No ma'am.

Did you just *ma'am* me??

Sure did.

Lol!

Guess all that shame you were feeling is gone out the window . . .

They're full on *bantering*, as Niecey would put it. Which is surprising to Leigh. It generally takes her a solid few weeks of interacting with someone to drop her guard.

And yet.

She steps onto the moving sidewalk that will carry her through the jungle. Decides to take a video, and focuses the camera on the illuminated ceiling.

Her phone buzzes again, and she almost drops it.

How bout you shush and gimme the next hint so we can get a move on here.

Oh.

(Leigh really did forget about the game for a minute.)

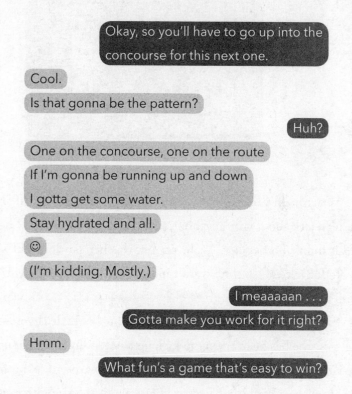

Leigh steps off the conveyor, pauses to jot down the next hint, and then shoots up the escalator steps, two at a time, into concourse B. Harper's moving too fast. Maybe Leigh should've done more than one clue in each concourse . . .

I'm up in A now.

Let's hear that hint, shall we?

Okay:

In the place where you find (Simply) paper plus ink lies a tale that for decades has made people think. A Scout and her Boo through all kinds of weather, the author is our two names taken together.

Okay, now you're just showing off.

Jabari hadn't been interested in Leigh's writing. At all. He wasn't a jerk about it or anything, just . . . indifferent. And Leigh *said* it didn't bother her. Yeah, poetry was her passion, but she wrote for herself, so if he wasn't interested, who cared, right? It wasn't about him.

Except now, with Harper complimenting her little rhymes—that yes, she has been trying to kick up a notch since *you certainly know how to turn a phrase*—Leigh wonders if maybe it *did* bother her that Jabari couldn't have cared less about the thing that was most important to her.

As a matter of fact, something about being away from the overwhelming whiteness of campus—from the buildings to the linens to the snow to the students and faculty—and surrounded by people of other races here in the Atlanta airport is making Leigh realize that perhaps a *lot* of things she says don't bother her actually do.

She stops to look out one of the wide windows. All is still outside except for the snow, which is coming down with force in fat, clumped flakes.

She pulls her phone from her pocket.

> So you go to school here in Atlanta?

There's a pause and then:

> Yo, I was just about to text you . . .
>
> Hold that thought for onnnnne sec
>
> . . .

A video appears in the message thread. Leigh's still got her headphones on, so the minute she hits play, a smooth, rich voice—makes her think of chocolate fondue—fills her ears and shoots a tingle down her arms and legs.

"*I like what you did with the word* simply," the voice says as the sign for Simply Books comes into view. "*You're clever, Miss Leigh. Real clever.*"

Leigh grins.

The video pans around the little airport bookstore, and the voice continues: "*This place is cute! OH, yo, have you read this yet?*" Zooms in on a book spine: *Exit West.* "*It's SO GOOD, Leigh. Matter of fact, I'm buying it for you.*" A brown hand appears and pulls the book from the shelf. "*Moving on, then*," the voice goes on. "*Time to find this clue. Hmmmm . . .*" The video moves around the store for about thirty seconds with Harper saying, "*Nope. Not here*," and then lands on someone up in a red apron on a ladder stocking books on the uppermost shelves.

"*Excuse me, ma'am*," Harper says. "*Could you tell me where to find the book* To Kill a Mockingbird*?*"

"Hey, that's cheating!" Leigh says. Aloud. In concourse B.

Heads turn. (Oops.)

Leigh shifts her attention back to the video and picks up her pace. Gotta get downstairs to find the next clue.

She watches the bookseller lead Harper to a table in the back corner where *To Kill a Mockingbird* is on display with a bunch of other "Classics." That same brown hand from before lifts the book from the table and holds it up in for the camera.

"*Wham bam*," the voice says.

And then the video cuts off.

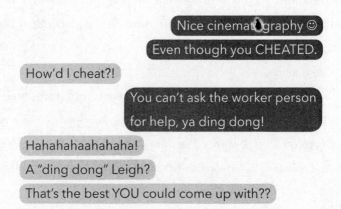

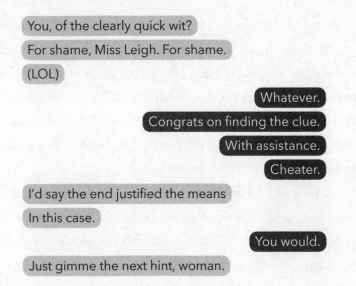

You, of the clearly quick wit?

For shame, Miss Leigh. For shame.

(LOL)

Whatever.

Congrats on finding the clue.

With assistance.

Cheater.

I'd say the end justified the means

In this case.

You would.

Just gimme the next hint, woman.

On her way down the escalator, Leigh spots a young man headed up, his arm draped over the shoulders of a blonde girl. He looks so much like Jabari—same deep brown skin the color of coffee beans, same cleft chin, same prep-swag style: plaid button-down, puffer vest, nice slacks, Air Jordans (which works somehow)—for a second, she can't breathe.

He lifts his chin at her in greeting as they pass each other (*whoops . . . was she staring?*) and Leigh gets slammed with some of the intense emotion she fights to suppress at school, but doesn't have it in her to keep in check now.

While the whole school "grieved" over the end of #Lebari, it didn't take long for Jabari to pop up on social media in photos with different girls who'd definitely wanted him while he was with her—and clearly weren't *that* sad about him being available again.

It was the strangest thing: No, she wasn't actually into him, but that didn't make it sting any less to see him with other girls. Not because she wanted him back. That wasn't it at all. It was more the fact that . . . well, nobody else at that school seemed to want *her*. Jabari was treated like a celebrated warrior returned from a brutal yet victorious battle, but Leigh was just some piteous castaway.

At least *with* Jabari she felt like she was a part of something. There were a lot of things they connected on, being two of only six black kids in their graduating class (Niecey was the third, Zuri the fourth, and the other two were a set of identical twins who through four years of high school really only seemed to interact with each other). When she and Jabari were together, Leigh's guard—that thing inside her that lowered her sensitivity and raised the armor that helped her cope when surrounded by people with more power than she had, but who were oblivious to the differences in their experiences—would fall away of its own accord.

Jabari just *got it*. Even more so than Niecey, who didn't come from a ton of money like Leigh and Jabari did. *She* didn't get that "being rich" doesn't really make being a token more comfortable. Matter of fact, if Leigh had a dollar for every kid who'd assumed she was there on scholarship, she'd be well on her way to covering a year's worth of her own tuition.

Her phone buzzes.

Leigh? You still there?

And then again, this time from Niecey (speak of the devil):

So? How goes it?

Leigh responds to Niecey first.

Goes great.

Actually having fun.

Sweet!

You meet her yet?

Again, I mean.

Nah, not yet.

I'll keep you posted.

She takes a deep breath before responding to Harper.

SO sorry.

Saw someone who looks like my very recent
ex on the escalator, and it threw me.

Can we umm . . . take a water break?

For a sec?

Yeah, of course.

You all right?

Yeah, I'm fine.

Just gotta get my head back in the game.

Gotcha.

Leigh steps into the tunnel between concourses B and C and is suddenly immersed in a history of Atlanta. She strolls slowly, taking in the timeline and reading some of the plaques. Being from up north, her knowledge of "Southern" history is cursory at best. Limited to what's in her textbooks. Seeing pictures of Civil War history and freed slaves, segregated lunch counters and Civil Rights marches, makes things *real* in a way Leigh's never experienced. And maybe it's just because she's wide open right now, but this visual representation of *her* people's history makes her feel grounded—*connected*—to something much bigger and more powerful than she.

After finding the next clue—a photo of the city post–Great Atlanta Fire of 1917—Leigh heads up the escalator into concourse C and drops down into a seat at the first gate she sees.

Her phone buzzes.

Sorry about the breakup.

From Harper.

It makes Leigh smile.

Nah, it's fine. Really wasn't that big a deal.

We were together for a minute but between you and me, I wasn't really that into it.

Wow, I've literally told NO ONE that and here I am telling you, person I haven't seen or spoken to in over a quarter of a decade?

Lol!

Makes sense if you think about it.

Who better to spill your guts to than someone uninvolved who you can't see?

True.

Didn't think of it that way.

To be honest, I kinda feel relieved. Letting that out.

So thanks.

☺

No problem.

So what was the issue with him if you don't mind my asking?

Or her.

Or them.

Let me not be over here assuming . . .

(Was that a hint? Maybe Harper *does* remember . . . Or maybe Leigh's overthinking again. This secrecy thing is exhausting.)

215

...

¯_(ツ)_/¯

Guess I just . . . wasn't that into him

Ha!

I've definitely been THERE.

You have?

Oh yeah.

Few times.

Honestly, it's not even the breakup that bothers me.

It's more like . . .

The aftermath. At school.

What's your school like?

It's here in Atlanta, right

Yeah.

Braselton Preparatory Academy.

(It's just as snooty-booty as it sounds.)

(Barf.)

Mine is pretty bad too.

"The Evanscroft School of Northampton"

(rolls eyes)

What's your black kid percentage?

Overall?

There are 23 of us in a school of 500.

So 4.6%

Damn.

Still better than mine.

18 in 439. 4.1%

And it's getting worse because 7 of those are in my graduating class.

The other 11 are sprinkled throughout the other three grades.

Like little specks of pepper on a heaping plate of fettuccine alfredo.

Lol!

An apt description for sure.

I'm actually glad to hear your school is just as bad as mine.

Nice knowing someone can relate.

My folks sure don't get it.

"This is an excellent opportunity, Harper."

UGH!

I KNOW RIGHT??

"It's the perfect launching pad into a bright future, Leigh."

This one time in tenth grade, the Swag Seven, as we call ourselves, got called to the office and questioned about why we all chose to sit together in the cafeteria.

"We're worried about this self-segregation," the headmaster said.

OMG.

MY crew was told that we were "making people feel unsafe."

As FRESHMEN.

Smh.

Ridiculous.

THAT'S what was so hard about the break up.

I'm suddenly like . . . alone again?

He's a dude, and a popular one at that.

So there are (white) girls all over him all the time.

I feel bad for saying that, but it's true.

Oh, I KNOW it's true.

Same at my school.

Meanwhile I'm just . . . there.

I mean, I'm not TOTALLY alone.

Niecey, my best friend at school, is black.

But like . . .

She has it in her head that because my parents are "successful" I shouldn't have any problems.

Like money can solve racism.

Though I do feel strange calling it racism.

Nobody's calling me the n-word or anything like that . . .

Oh, it's definitely racism.

The systemic type.

Don't even get me started.

Tbh, the hardest thing about being in boarding school in the South is the sheer number of people who like to pretend racism isn't a *thing* anymore.

Just know that discomfort you feel is mad valid. You're not being "too sensitive."

You're not "overreacting."

Racism is built into the foundations of this country.

So it definitely affects how people see and interact with each other.

Getting off my soapbox now.

Sorry about that, lol.

Don't be.

It's . . . exactly what I needed to hear, I think.

So thank you.

You're welcome.

Miss Leigh ☺

. . .

Wow, things got a little heavy there for a sec, huh?

Lol, you could say that.

Ready for that next clue?

Bring it.

K.

ahem

Between A and B, a rainforest thrives filled with lights, sights, sounds, and fake fireflies. As you stroll, look around. Even up at the sky. You might find a great flock with wings spread, flying high.

These just keep getting better.

I feel like I'm going through one of those I SPY books for real.

Leigh smiles harder than she has in quite some time but doesn't respond. Just slides down in the chair and exhales. As her eyes roam the space around gate C22, she notices things she's sure she'd normally miss: a businessman furiously typing away on an iPad with an attachable keyboard; a mom pacing back and forth as she bounces a baby in her arms; two little black girls playing a hand game like the ones Leigh used to play with her cousins; a pair of ladies huddled in a corner, giggling over a magazine . . .

Her eyes stick there.

One woman is brown-skinned, with her hair cut so low, she's almost bald, and the other is lighter, with big curly hair. And there's a vibe, a rhythm, between them that makes it clear they're more than friends. It's in the way they smile at each other and brush hands and lean in so close, there's no doubt they can each smell what the other ate for dinner.

Leigh has no idea what they're looking at, but suddenly buzz-cut lady's mouth drops open and she swats curly lady on the arm with the back of her hand. Curly lady throws her head back in laughter while buzz-cut lady pouts, then curly lady leans over to whisper something in buzz-cut lady's ear—something that turns buzz-cut lady's scowl into a smile.

They kiss, and Leigh quickly looks away.

Her phone buzzes, and it startles her so bad, she leaps to her feet.

Which draws the attention of the lady couple. Buzz-cut lady smiles at Leigh . . . and warmth spreads through Leigh's chest like she's just taken a big gulp of hot cocoa. She feels . . . seen.

In a good way.

She smiles back and heads up the concourse in search of the next clue.

❄   ❄   ❄

The message attached to the photo of the digital sky in the middle of the airport jungle makes Leigh laugh aloud:

> Bruh, I just want you to know I stood here staring up at this thing for a solid 5 minutes before remembering I needed to take a picture.

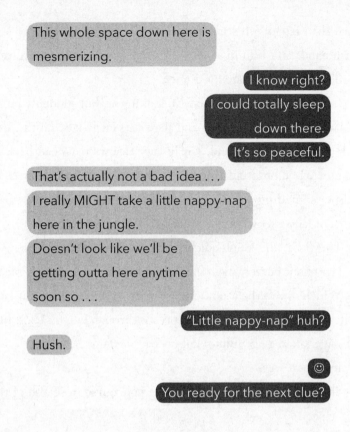

This whole space down here is mesmerizing.

I know right?

I could totally sleep down there.

It's so peaceful.

That's actually not a bad idea . . .

I really MIGHT take a little nappy-nap here in the jungle.

Doesn't look like we'll be getting outta here anytime soon . . .

"Little nappy-nap" huh?

Hush.

☺

You ready for the next clue?

Because Leigh finds she's certainly ready to give it. As a matter of fact, there's a part of her that's ready for this game to end so she can *see* Harper. Not that she fully understands why.

Concourse B, right?

Actually, don't answer that.

Hit me.

☺

> Near the second alpha letter and the number after ten works a very lively bearded man who has a lot of friends; he hands out wheat hydration so he'll never be alone; the place of Sugar H2O is where he makes his home.

On it.

> I'll give you the next one too.

> Fifty-two years after slaves were made free, a city was razed by "hot" powers that be. It raged and devoured all things in its wake; the only thing worse would've been an earthquake.

☺

Cute.

Man, B11 is FAR.

You got me out here trekking to the ends of the earth and stuff . . .

> I literally just snorted.

> AND found the next clue just now.

How many are there gonna be?

We going up and down all the way through concourse E?

Which . . . is a good question. On the one hand, Leigh's ready to *see* Harper. Make herself the final clue and be done with it. (But is that too presumptuous?)

What she really wants to do is sit down with Harper and just tell her everything: how wildly alone she feels at school (and not just because of the race thing); how intensely attracted she is to Zuri (though she would *never* tell her); how she thinks she might like girls and how much that scares her because one area of overt marginalization is quite enough, thank you very much.

She just wants to unload. Get it all out.

Maybe she will just plop down at one of these gates and make herself the next clue.

But could she really say everything she wants to Harper's face?

What does Harper's face even look like now?

Leigh honestly *should* know. There's no doubt Harper Kemp's on "social media," as adults like to put it. In fact, Leigh thought about looking up Harper the moment Mama and Daddy told Leigh about Christmas in Florida.

But she couldn't bring herself to do it. Not with the breakup and the questions and the Zuri thing. At that point, seeing the first girl Leigh ever *noticed* noticed would've been waaaay too much.

But what about now?

Her phone buzzes.

"Sugar H2O"

The Sweet Water Draft House

Hella clever, Miss Leigh.

And then the picture. Of the bearded bartender double-fisting goblets of beer with the biggest, brightest smile on his face.

Leigh almost can't take it.

> Headed down the escalator now.
>
> On to the next one
>
> ☺

Leigh's not ready.

She rushes back toward the center of the concourse— hurriedly picking the weakest/wackest clue yet—and flies down the concourse C escalator in hopes of disappearing into the tunnel that leads to concourse D before Harper sends her the next picture. Leigh's sure it won't take very long.

> Next hint!
>
> While typically known as a beacon of death who sings to poor sailors thus stealing their breath, the good ol US sees me more as a queen and puts me all over their cups of caffeine.
>
> Perfect timing!

A photo comes through of the plaque in the *Walk Through Atlanta History* exhibit that details the Great Atlanta Fire of 1917.

This whole thing is pretty dope.

Got Dr. King down here.

Details about the Native American tribes that used to reside in this area.

Brief history of Coca-Cola.

Wild. (And dope.)

Yep.

When Leigh lifts her eyes, she's reached the tunnel.

And it's empty.

No art. No cool lights. No history exhibit.

Just moving sidewalks lining bare concrete walls that glow a sickly off-white from the fluorescent ceiling lights.

Part of her is so disappointed she doesn't even want to walk through it.

Except Harper's catching up to her.

She jets through and up into concourse D.

I have some sad news.

Ruh-roh . . .

(Leigh pretends the Scooby-Doo reference doesn't make her stomach somersault in the most delightful way possible. She and Harper watched a *lot* of Scooby-Doo after kid-curfew on that cruise. Does Harper remember, or was that random?)

> There's nothing between C and D.
> Like . . . literally nothing.

Well . . .

A photo of the infamous (according to Leigh's hyper-bougie, "pour-over only" drinking parents at least) green Starbucks siren appears beneath Harper's previous message.

Since I'm here . . .

I'm gonna just grab and bite and a beverage.

You want something?

> Preciate it, but no thanks.
> ☺

You mind if I take a minute to eat?

Ya girl is famished.

Lol.

(True though.)

> Take your time.

Sweet.

Thanks.

> . . .
> Hey Harper?
> Can I ask you something?

HA!

You just did, sucka.

LOL!

You can ask me something else though.

☺

You're silly.

Guilty.

Now what's the question?

Leigh sighs.

Okay . . .

So this might sound a bit dramatic . . .

But have you ever felt like . . .

There's just no place for you in this world?

Sorry. I know that's like deeply philosophical or whatever . . .

Don't apologize.

I feel that way all the time, Leigh.

You do?

Yep.

Will it offend you if I say I'm relieved?

LOL!

Nah.

I'm glad you are.

Nice to know you're not alone right?

> Yeah. Exactly that.

> You're really easy to talk to.

Yeah?

> Yeah.

> Maybe it's what you said before . . .

> Your uninvolved invisibility.

Lol

> But . . .

> I kinda feel like I could tell you anything?

> Which is a little bit scary for me.

Why's that?

(You absolutely CAN tell me anything by the way.)

(I like to think myself a pretty good secret keeper.)

(Not to toot my own horn or anything.)

(Side note: this double-smoked bacon sandwich is lit.)

(You sure you don't want one?)

(Not to change the subject . . . my bad.)

> (Lol, it's cool.)

> (I'm really not hungry, but thanks.)

> (Getting back to the subject at hand . . .)

I think it's scary because I'm so used to having my guard up. Protecting myself.

Makes sense.

Can I . . . tell you something else?

That I haven't told anyone?

Course you can, Leigh.

You won't judge me?

I think that might be my greatest fear, by the way.

Even though I know other people's judgments don't REALLY matter . . .

(Or so my mama says)

. . .

I dunno

I guess since I ALWAYS feel like I'm being judged . . .

Watched with a critical eye . . .

Everyone waiting for me to make a mistake . . .

Yep.

I get it.

Trust me.

The pressure is real, man.

YES.

IT IS

Okay so . . .

The REAL reason my ex and I fell apart is . . .

Well . . .

I think I might not be totally . . . into . . . people . . . like him.

What type of people is that?

Mmmm . . .

Well there was this . . . girl?

Ah.

Okay.

Go on.

Ugh.

I can't believe I'm telling you this.

Telling ANYONE this.

. . .

Her name is Zuri.

That's a gorgeous name.

It's . . . fitting.

Lol.

Nice.

And I kept having these . . . thoughts. Of her.

About her.

Thoughts?

Like . . .

Intimate ones?

231

Not even on purpose

They would like . . . pop into my head unbidden.

I see.

And I think my boyfriend could tell

That I'd like . . . lost interest

Makes sense.

I've never even spoken to this girl by the way.

I just gawp from a distance like a creep

Hahaha!

Been there. Trust.

So ridiculous.

You feel better though, right?

Having gotten that out?

I do

Lighte

Good.

So how bout that next hint?

Oh . . .

Lol, I need to find a clue

Hold that though

Leigh looks all around and catches sight of something twinkling in the light. *Many* things twinkling.

A Swarovski store.

Leigh smiles the biggest smile she's smiled all day.

On day three of the cruise, she and Harper bought matching charm bracelets from a Swarovski store in the ship's shopping atrium.

And Leigh's never taken hers off.

She tugs her sleeve back and reaches for her wrist as her brain tries to pull together a hint—maybe she'll stand across from the store and have something in there that'll make Harper turn around and see her—

Her arm is bare.

The bracelet is gone.

> Hey, we gotta pause the game.
>
> Maybe indefinitely?

Oh no . . .

What happened?

> I think I lost something. Though
> I'm not sure how or where.
>
> Ugh.

What is it?

Maybe I can help you look?

I've been just about everywhere
you have, right?

> You remember when we bought
> those Swarovski charm bracelets?

I do.

> You still have yours?

There's a ". . ." and then a photo of a silver bracelet with six charms dangling from it—attached to a key ring with four keys and two other keychains—appears on Leigh's phone screen.

You added to yours!

Yeah.

You haven't?

No.

And now I dunno if I'll ever be able to because that's what I lost.

Oh man

Where'd you last have it?

I mean . . .

I never take it off.

Actually wait! I DID take it off.

To go through security.

Okay so we have a last-sighting.

This is good.

You remember where you put it?

I do.

In the mesh pocket on the side of my backpack.

. . .

Which I just checked.

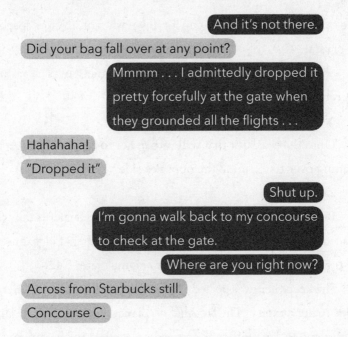

And it's not there.

Did your bag fall over at any point?

Mmmm . . . I admittedly dropped it
pretty forcefully at the gate when
they grounded all the flights . . .

Hahahaha!

"Dropped it"

Shut up.

I'm gonna walk back to my concourse
to check at the gate.

Where are you right now?

Across from Starbucks still.

Concourse C.

Which is precisely where Leigh needs to go. Definitely not
ready to see Harper *now*, so . . .

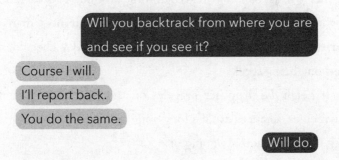

Will you backtrack from where you are
and see if you see it?

Course I will.

I'll report back.

You do the same.

Will do.

Leigh retraces her steps back into to the tunnels—spending
the entirety of the escalator ride down leaning over the railing so

she can check the side going up for any flashes of silver or sparkles of crystal.

She walks back along the lifeless tunnel, eyes scanning, searching, watching.

Nothing.

Onto the escalator that will return her to concourse C. Again leaning over to examine the opposite side.

Zilch.

Back along the path to Starbucks—though Harper totally just traced this way so it's probably pointless—then Leigh busts a U-turn and makes a beeline for her original gate: C42.

She keeps her eyes peeled the whole walk there, which merely adds to her anxiety: The fact that no planes are taking off or landing seems to have officially caused an *increase* in the amount of activity within the airport—people coming, going, sitting, standing. There's a group with instruments out jamming and another group dancing. Kids running around. People talking, laughing, gathering in the concourse restaurants, drinking. Christmas lights and giant ornaments and holiday cheer despite everyone being stuck.

If Leigh *did* drop her bracelet on the way to start hunting down clues, chances are it's long gone now. How could it not be with this much activity going on?

She reaches the gate. Looks around the area where she was sitting.

Nothing.

Goes to the counter to ask if anyone turned a bracelet in.

Nope.

Leigh returns to her original seat and takes a deep breath.
Pulls out her phone.

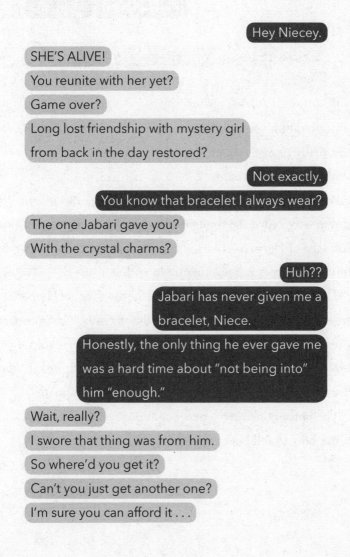

Hey Niecey.

SHE'S ALIVE!

You reunite with her yet?

Game over?

Long lost friendship with mystery girl
from back in the day restored?

Not exactly.

You know that bracelet I always wear?

The one Jabari gave you?

With the crystal charms?

Huh??

Jabari has never given me a
bracelet, Niece.

Honestly, the only thing he ever gave me
was a hard time about "not being into"
him "enough."

Wait, really?

I swore that thing was from him.

So where'd you get it?

Can't you just get another one?

I'm sure you can afford it . . .

Leigh bites her tongue.

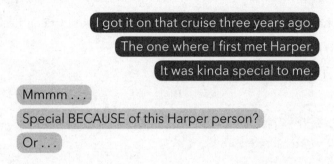

> I got it on that cruise three years ago.
>
> The one where I first met Harper.
>
> It was kinda special to me.

Mmmm . . .

Special BECAUSE of this Harper person?

Or . . .

Leigh doesn't respond immediately. She can't. In truth, she's never really thought about *why* she always kept the bracelet on. It was always just . . . there.

But it's a good question. *Why* was it so special to Leigh? Why is she so wrecked at the thought of losing it? No, she doesn't think it's *because* of Harper—but she also can't say with complete certainty that Harper has nothing to do with it.

There's no denying that cruise, and the discovery of Harper's . . . Harperness, were formative for Leigh in some way. That something shifted back then and despite three years of trying to keep it suppressed, it's obviously blossomed in some way. Expanded where other things—like Leigh's interest in guys—has contracted.

The bracelet marked a new beginning.

But how to tell Niecey that?

> Hey Niece?

Present.

I need to tell you something.

Clearly.

I've been waiting for a response for three minutes now.

Rude.

This is kind of a serious thing . . .

Don't be a drama queen, L-Dub.

What is it?

Here goes . . .

Well, just coming right out with it . . .

(No pun intended, but #fitting)

I think I might be gay.

Oh.

Are you . . .

Secretly in love with me then?

WHAT?!

NO!

Hahahahaha!

I know you're not in love with me.

Just trying to, ya know . . .

Break the rainbow ice or whatever.

I don't care if you're gay, Leigh.

Oh.

I mean unless you're planning to ditch me for some girl who will make out with you . . .

Lo

Honestly, it's still too new

Too much to figure ou

Though I think I realized it a long time ago

Harper?

Yeah

Makes sense.

So you gonna avoid her til kingdom come now?

Actually you still really can't, can you?

Not really

And I mean . . .

Maybe I don't want to

Avoid her I mean

LE PLOT THICKENS!

Shut up

She actually just texted again

I'll be right back, k'

Kk.

Leigh switches over to Harper's messages.

No-go anywhere between the Atlanta History stroll and the jungle.

> You didn't take the train at all, right?

No

> Okay. I'll keep looking.

Leigh sighs.

There's a part of her deep down that knows it's a lost cause.

A part that wants Harper to give it up and come find her.

And another part that doesn't want that at all.

That feels too open.

Too vulnerable.

She just told two people something that literally changes the entire trajectory of her life. Is she ready to look one of them in the face?

Leigh slouches down in the seat, closes her eyes, and lets her head fall back.

It's all so . . . much.

What will her parents say?

And people at school?

"Excuse me, Miss?"

Leigh startles and jerks upright.

"Oh man, I'm sorry. Didn't mean to scare you. You just, umm . . ." The person—a girl—unslings her backpack and squats down to riffle around inside it. "Sorry, one sec. I had it right here . . ."

As the girl searches, Leigh takes her in: She seems tall, though Leigh can't be sure with her squatting now. Slim, but clearly athletic if the strong shoulders are any indication. Brown skin. Shoulder-length dreadlocks. Gray beanie. Kinda tomboyish.

"Aha!" she says.

And she pulls out Leigh's bracelet.

"This fell out of your bag when you left the gate area a while back," she says. "Been waiting for you to return so I could give it to you."

"Oh my god!" Leigh takes the bracelet and holds it up to the light. "I can't even believe it," she whispers.

She immediately grabs her phone to text Harper:

> You'll never believe it . . .
>
> Someone just returned my bracelet to me!

A *ping* noise sounds, followed closely by a second one.

The girl in front of Leigh pulls a phone out of her pocket and begins to tap out a message.

Which is when Leigh finally looks at her face.

Leigh's phone buzzes in her hand.

New message from Harper.

> You're welcome.
>
> ☺

Leigh's head snaps up.

The girl—definitely, definitely Harper—is still tapping away on her phone.

Another buzz.

> Don't be mad but . . .
>
> I actually saw it fall outta your bag.
>
> My gate was the one across the way.
>
> Flight canceled earlier in the day.
>
> Got rebooked on yours, in fact, but we see how that went, lol.

(Leigh wants to respond, but her thumbs are frozen.)

> I recognized you the moment you arrived at the gate.
>
> Just as gorgeous as I remembered.
>
> (Might've had a little crush on you when we were fourteen . . .)

When Leigh looks up this time, Harper's staring at her.
Smiling.
Leigh smiles back.
Then picks up her phone.

> It was definitely mutual.

No text response, but Leigh can tell from the way Harper looks shyly away that she's . . . pleased.

> So . . .
>
> What now?
>
> Maybe a little I Spy?
>
> Hide and Seek?
>
> Silent Assassins?

>> Huh??

> Just kidding about that last one.
>
> Lol.

>> I'm dead.
>>
>> Get it?

Harper snorts and finally stuffs her phone in her pocket. "Still telling them wack behind jokes, I see," she says, extending a hand.

Leigh swats it away and gets to her feet. "Umm excuse you, my jokes are not wack."

"Oh yes they are," Harper says as Leigh settles her backpack on her shoulders and the girls fall into synchronized step (and right back into their fourteen-year-old-girl rapport). "Remember that pirate one you told me when we were hiding in that one corridor on the cruise ship, determined to sneak into the engine room—"

"Which was locked down tighter than—"

"Bellatrix Lestrange's Gringotts vault," the girls finish together before exploding into laughter.

"Bro, what were we even thinking?" Harper says, shaking her head.

Leigh has tears streaming down her face she's laughing so hard. "I mean . . . *were* we thinking?"

"Probably not. Though I'm pretty sure the whole thing was *your* idea."

"Likely." Leigh wipes her face. Looking around, there's no denying the twinkling lights seem brighter and the decorations more vibrant. She glances out one of the massive windows, and the snowflakes are so thick, they look like bizarrely lightweight sugar cubes . . . but despite knowing that means they're likely not getting out anytime soon, she can't help but marvel at the wonder that is nature in this moment.

She looks at Harper in profile and her heart does a little tap dance.

Leigh clears her throat and turns away. "I'll have you know that pirate joke has made me quite the hit at rich, drunken white kid parties. *Ahem* . . . What, I ask you, is a pirate's favorite letter?"

"Oh god, here we go . . ."

(Leigh can practically *hear* Harper's eyes rolling.)

"You'd think *R-rrrr* . . . but a pirate's first love is the *C*!"

"Jesus, Mary, and Joseph."

"Don't forget Abraham."

"I'm dead." And Harper busts up in another spurt of laughter.

"Hmph. Calling *me* wack. Though fine, the engine room break-in was a fairly wack idea."

"And my dumb self went right along with it."

"Sure did."

"I'll be honest with you, though," Harper says, "if you would've suggested we try to scale that weird red-and-blue tail-looking thing on the top deck to take our stand as cruise ship conquerors, I would've immediately tried to figure out the physics. You had ya girl *wrapped*."

Leigh has no clue how to respond to that.

"Also: where are we even going?" Harper looks around.

Leigh starts laughing again. "If I recall correctly, you pulled *me* out of *my* seat and started walking."

"I . . . can't argue with that," Harper says. "Okay, stop." And she puts a hand on Leigh's shoulder.

So they do. In the middle of the concourse atrium.

There's a lady playing an electric violin—"Let It Snow" with a little hip hoppish flair—and people continue to flow around them. Normally, this would make Leigh cringe, being in a position that makes her so conspicuous. But right now? With Harper Kemp beside her and so much life and breath and happy holiday magic pulsating around them? Well, she's in no rush to move.

Move they do, though:

"I've got it!" Harper says. And she grabs Leigh's hand and pulls her toward the escalators.

❄ ❄ ❄

Who-knows-how-many IHOP pancakes (they had an unlimited thing going on) and a trip *back* through the security checkpoint (they had to exit to get to the airport IHOP) later, Leigh and Harper pop into a concourse T souvenir shop to buy tacky and overpriced *Atlanta* fleece blankets and those bizarre, though surprisingly effective, U-shaped neck pillows.

Then they head down into the airport jungle.

"This is fine, right?" Leigh says, dropping her backpack against one of the walls and plopping down beside it, crisscross-applesauce.

Harper follows suit, propping her bag against the wall and stretching out to lean her shoulders back against it. She tucks her neck pillow into place. "We stuck here, so might as well kick it where we want to, right?"

"Fair point." Leigh relaxes back herself and stares up at the faux-forest canopy above them. "It really is beautiful down here, huh?"

Harper doesn't respond, and when Leigh looks down to find out why, Harper is staring. At Leigh.

Grinning.

Leigh gulps and tries to tuck a strand of her massive hair behind her ear.

"It's really good to see you, man," Harper says. "I can't even tell you the number of times I almost followed you on Insta and Snap, but stopped myself."

This surprises Leigh. "Really?"

"Yeah. I umm . . ." Harper shifts her gaze away. "Well on the cruise, you kinda ghosted after that day at the pool, so like—I dunno. I guess I was worried I'd been overzealous with my crush or something. That it'd wigged you out."

"Wait, for real?"

"Uhh . . . yeah. I basically followed you around like a puppy from the moment we boarded the ship. I didn't wanna seem like a creep online—even though I *did* wanna see you."

Leigh is floored. "When did you know?" she asks before she can catch herself.

"Huh?"

Leigh takes a deep breath. "When did you know you . . . liked girls?"

"Oh, pretty much always." Harper waves the awkwardness of the question away. "When we'd role-play in kindergarten, I wouldn't participate unless I was allowed to be the second mom. And I just *knew* I was gonna marry this red-haired, freckled black girl in my class named Imani. I had our babies' names picked out and everything."

"Wow."

"Can I say something?"

"Of course."

Harper sits up and shifts so she can look Leigh in the eye.

And now their knees are touching.

(Leigh thinks she might be dying.)

"Just want you to know I'm here for you, Leigh-ski."

Leigh is *officially* dead now. That's what Harper used to call her back in the day.

Leigh gulps. "Okay."

"Any questions, comments, concerns, you let me know."

"What are you, a flight attendant?"

Both girls laugh and the tension breaks.

"I really do appreciate that, Harper. It's admittedly a lot. This . . . shift."

"It is."

"My turn to tell *you* something now," Leigh goes on.

Harper smiles (and Leigh's stomach swoops like the flock of birds on the digital jungle sky). "I'm listening."

"So the whole cruise thing—" *Is she really about to say this?* "Well the reason I *ghosted*, as you so aptly put it, is because I . . . uhh . . . well, let's just say you're the first girl I ever noticed. In that way."

Harper's drops her chin, but Leigh can tell she's smiling.

"And like, I thought you noticed me . . . noticing you. And maybe weren't okay with it?"

"Ah."

"I was embarrassed," Leigh goes on.

Harper's eyes lift and lock onto Leigh's again—

And then someone shouts "*Merry Christmas to all!*" jolting both of them out of what was a certifiable Moment. They look up just as a skinny guy in an oversized Santa suit steps onto the moving sidewalk, waving like he's Miss America.

"Bro, I can't," Harper says, and they both collapse into side-splitting laughter.

❀   ❀   ❀

They talk.

And talk.

And laugh.

And talk.

The snow stops (or so they hear from passersby).

Touching knees become melded sides become Harper's arm around Leigh's shoulders and Leigh's cheek against Harper's clavicle.

Hands find their way together.

More talking. Laughing. Smiling. Reminiscing.

Learning.

Growing.

(Re)Connecting.

Eyes meet.

Time slows.

Noses touch.

Lips collide.

❀   ❀   ❀

Niecey-Poo?

You awake?

"Be right back" my ass . . .

250

It's 1 a.m.!

Ugh.

I'm sorry.

Whatever, loser.

I'll forgive you this time.

You're in the midst of an identity crisis, so.

You get a pass.

Just don't let it happen again.

Lol, shut up.

So what's the latest?

Got my bracelet back!

Sweeeeet!

That's amazing.

You meet up with Harper?

...

Leigh!

Huh?

SPILL.

I mean . . .

We met.

And???

☺☺☺

LEIGH DANIELLE WELLS!

GET TO TALKING THIS INSTANT!

Merry Christmas, Niece.

❊   ❊   ❊

As Leigh steps out of the plane-to-gate tunnel into Palm Beach International airport, Harper Kemp smiles at her and steps forward with her hand extended. The two girls weren't able get on the same flight out of Atlanta once the ground stop was lifted, but now here they are. Together again.

Their fingers entwine.

"I missed you, Leigh-ski," Harper says, kissing Leigh on the cheek.

Leigh giggles.

As they make their way toward baggage claim to meet both sets of parents, Leigh's heart speeds up. She knows Harper is out to her folks ("Though I've never brought a girl home. Til now, hadn't met one worth bringing.")—which likely means Leigh's parents also know Harper's gay. But Leigh'd be lying if she said she wasn't nervous about what Tisha and David Wells will say/ think about *their* daughter's . . . new status.

"I have a joke," Harper says.

And Leigh smiles and exhales. Gives Harper's hand a little squeeze of appreciation.

Harper squeezes back. "You ready?"

"Hit me."

"What did the fish say when he swam into the concrete wall?"

"Mmmm . . ."

"DAM!"

Leigh snorts.

The exit doors loom large.

"Wait," and Leigh stops walking. Harper jolts back, and Leigh looks down at their interlinked fingers.

Harper turns to face Leigh. Lifts Leigh's chin with her free hand and looks straight into Leigh's brown eyes. "You sure about this?" And Harper lifts their linked hands. "You know we can keep it between us for now. Walk out as old homies. The parents don't *need* to know at this point."

Leigh's eyes trace over Harper's face. She takes the whole glorious package in. "I *want* them to know, Harp."

"Yeah?" (And there's that smile Leigh loves so, so much.)

"Yeah. This is the happiest I've been in a long time. It's a little scary, yeah. But . . . it's good. We're good. *You're* good."

"You think I'm good, huh?" Harper's eyes drop to Leigh's lips.

"Yeah. I do."

"Dope." Another smile. "So you ready?"

Leigh looks at the automatic doors that will release her and Harper into the world. As a . . . thing. A pair.

A couple?

A couple.

She doesn't speak. Just pulls Harper to the holly-trimmed exit and through the doors.

❄   ❄   ❄

(The parents are thrilled, by the way.)

About the Authors

Photo by Denise Bovee

MELISSA DE LA CRUZ is the #1 *New York Times* bestselling author of many critically acclaimed and award-winning novels for readers of all ages, including her most recent hits: Disney's Descendants series; the Blue Bloods series; the Witches of East End series (which was adapted into a two-season television drama on Lifetime); *Alex & Eliza: A Love Story*; *Something in Between*; and *Pride and Prejudice and Mistletoe*. Melissa is the codirector of YALLFest (Charleston, South Carolina) and the cofounder of YALLWest (Santa Monica, California). She grew up in Manila, and she now lives in West Hollywood, California, with her husband and daughter. Learn more at melissa-delacruz.com.

AIMEE FRIEDMAN is a *New York Times* bestselling author of several novels for young adults, including *Two Summers* and *Sea Change*, which was adapted into a television movie for Lifetime. Aimee also works as an editorial director at Scholastic Inc., where she edits books for young readers. Born to immigrant parents in Queens, New York, Aimee attended the Bronx High School of Science and Vassar College. She now lives, writes, and works in Manhattan, but loves to travel whenever she can. Learn more at aimeefriedmanbooks.com.

Photo by Nigel Livingstone

NIC STONE is the *New York Times* bestselling author of the novels *Dear Martin* and *Odd One Out*. She was born and raised in a suburb of Atlanta, Georgia, and the only thing she loves more than an adventure is a good story about one. After graduating from Spelman College, she worked extensively in teen mentoring and lived in Israel for a few years before returning to the US to write full-time. Growing up with a wide range of cultures, religions, and backgrounds, she strives to bring these diverse voices and stories to her work. Learn more at nicstone.info.

Photo by Stephanie Ryan Photography

KASIE WEST is the acclaimed author of ten YA novels, including *The Fill-In Boyfriend*, *P.S. I Like You*, *By Your Side*, *Lucky in Love*, and *Listen to Your Heart*. Her books have received numerous accolades and have been named as ALA Quick Picks for Reluctant Readers and as YALSA Best Books for Young Adults. Kasie lives in Fresno, California, with her family. Learn more at kasiewest.com.

POINT PAPERBACKS
THIS IS YOUR LIFE IN FICTION

**BOOKS ABOUT LIFE. BOOKS ABOUT LOVE.
BOOKS ABOUT YOU.**

IreadYA.com

POINT